G R JORDAN

Infiltrator

A Kirsten Stewart Thriller

First published by Carpetless Publishing 2023

First edition

ISBN: 978-1-915562-32-6

This book was professionally typeset on Reedsy.
Find out more at reedsy.com

What is told into the ear of a man is
often heard a hundred miles away.

UNKNOWN

Contents

Foreword

The events of this book, while based on places across the globe, including the UK, Argentina and Uruguay, are entirely fictional and all characters do not represent any living or deceased person.

Acknowledgement

To Ken, Jean, Colin, Evelyn, John and Rosemary for your work in bringing this novel to completion, your time and effort is deeply appreciated.

Novels by G R Jordan

The Highlands and Islands Detective series (Crime)

Kirsten Stewart Thrillers (Thriller)

The Contessa Munroe Mysteries (Cozy Mystery)

The Patrick Smythe Series (Crime)

1. The Disappearance of Russell Hadleigh
2. The Graves of Calgary Bay
3. The Fairy Pools Gathering

Austerley & Kirkgordon Series (Fantasy)

1. Crescendo!
2. The Darkness at Dillingham
3. Dagon's Revenge
4. Ship of Doom

Supernatural and Elder Threat Assessment Agency (SETAA) Series (Fantasy)

1. Scarlett O'Meara: Beastmaster

Island Adventures Series (Cosy Fantasy Adventure)

1. Surface Tensions

Dark Wen Series (Horror Fantasy)

1. The Blasphemous Welcome
2. The Demon's Chalice

Chapter 01

He had left the car off to the side of the road, where hopefully they wouldn't see it. The night was sultry. Sweating, he ran as hard as he could along the dusty track that serviced the Argentinian coastline. He was only a mile from the border with Uruguay, a border that split the middle of a tidal inlet. He could reach the fishing community that he was familiar with—small, but quiet at this time of night. His plan was to steal a fishing boat, a local one, small and inconspicuous. With darkness having fallen, only the single light shining from the boat would show its passage.

Franco Manfrin was a man almost out of time. If he could reach the other side, if he could get to a fishing port in Uruguay, then maybe his life would continue. He'd steal away even further. They would look after him once he got there, wouldn't they? After all, Godfrey had put him here. The tall Englishman who had found him, a not-so-chance meeting in a cafe in Buenos Aires, Godfrey had hired him to infiltrate.

What a tale he'd found during his work, but there was no time to think about that now. He carried it all in his head. He'd contacted by the usual drop method, a direct message to Godfrey requesting an urgent meeting. Of course, he wouldn't get Godfrey at first. He would get one of the lower-ranking officials, one of the British agents who simply sat and watched and ran the local networks. From there, once they heard what he was going to say, they would escalate quickly up the chain.

They'd fly him to the UK, or at least somewhere safer. He'd spend days in a debriefing room just to make sure that they'd egged everything out of him. Of course, they'd be cross-checking to make sure he hadn't been fed lies. Or that he hadn't turned. He hadn't.

The dust continued to rise as he ran, and he thought he could hear cars in the night. Out here amongst the trees, it was usually so quiet except for a possible engine in the distance; the river beside him was also quiet, languid. He hoped the channel would be the same. He wasn't the greatest fisherman and had only ever been on a boat in his early years, sailing for his father. But tonight, he would have to sail for his freedom.

Boats weren't difficult, were they? Certainly not the operation of them. You just started the engine, turned the radar, steered where you wanted to go. It was when the water got high, he worried. Nervous when the waters chopped here and there, pushing against the boat. In the dark, he'd have to navigate, but again, all he needed was a compass to point east. When he got to the other shoreline, he would head north or south, and find a port that'd be the one he knew.

Sometimes he wished he carried a gun, but that would be too suspicious. He tried to appear a bumbling fool, a threat to no one, and that had allowed him to get close. He appreciated how he could look inconspicuous. Often he appeared as that person in the background, the one nobody pays any attention to because, frankly, they're not capable of anything. Well, Franco was. Franco was very capable. If he could just find himself on the other side of this tidal inlet, he would be home free. He would've broken up one of the most damaging terrorist threats to Britain that had ever been known.

His shirt clung to him. The sweat from his body left it soaked, but Franco ignored that and cut off the road and the dusty stones until he was deep in scrubland. He was more used to city streets, happier operating there, but here was his bid for freedom. They were on to him. Finally, they'd broken him down. They'd seen that he wasn't the bumbling idiot he made out to be. Franco Manfrin, in some ways, was a genius, but they'd realised it. That was why his greatness was in doubt.

A little branch caught him in the face. Franco brushed off the sting and kept his legs pumping. He ducked around this tree and that, and eventually saw the wide expanse of the river ahead of him. Directly across was the Isla Juncal, an island that occasionally would disappear when the tide was high and flooding. In the weak moonlight, he thought he could see land. The most important question, though, was where was he on the banks of the Argentinian side?

He strode close to the river, looked left and looked right, and then headed north. It was round the corner, maybe three hundred metres away, but they were the longest three hundred metres of his life. He half expected to round the corner to see nothing there, but he saw the little jetty and three fishing boats. One was small and single person, and looked more easily handled than the other two.

Franco untied the mooring ropes, threw them onto the middle vessel, and jumped on board. He felt the boat rock slightly and took a moment to steady himself before entering the tiny wheelhouse. The keys were still there because no one here would take a boat. He was out in the middle of nowhere.

His heart breathed a sigh of relief as the engine spurted into life.

Franco turned the wheel, steering his little boat towards the Isla Juncal. He would round it on the south side, and from there, he could stay straight, whatever straight was. He would reach the Uruguayan side close to a familiar jetty. The key thing wasn't the jetty; it was the fact that he could jump into a taxi. All of six hundred yards beyond the jetty, there was a small town. Around this hour, some bars would still be open, still a lure for taxis to be waiting. Once in a taxi, he'd go to Montevideo and run into the British embassy.

Something clipped off the top of the wheelhouse. It must have been a shot. Was that it? The boat was rocked slightly by the impact, but not enough to affect him. Franco ducked down in the wheelhouse and the window in the wheelhouse's door blew out, glass spraying.

No! They'd seen him leave. They couldn't have. Still, he was on a boat. As long as they didn't follow.

He reached up to the control panel and switched off the single white navigation light at the top, but he could hear another boat starting. Shortly, as he looked behind him, he could see the faint outline of a bigger fishing boat coming for him.

Damn it, he needed to hold course. Thankfully, the inlet was not showing its strongest current, but looking at the Isla Juncal, he thought it to be small. Had the tide flooded? He hadn't checked the tidal charts because he'd had to get out of Buenos Aires so quickly. Never had he looked back. He hadn't waited for anyone, not even that rather pretty girl that he occasionally saw on a Friday night. He'd miss her.

Then something struck him. He was steering ahead for the

corner of the Isla Juncal. If the tide was high, if it was flooded and there wasn't much of the Isla Juncal, he'd have to steer on a wider course. How deep was the draught of the boat he was in? What clearance did he need from the silty mud below?

Franco did not know. He was in that precarious position of knowing of the possible dangers without having a clue or the information to work out whether they were truly dangerous. As he motored forward, his mind was suddenly taken from this distraction to a very prominent sound.

It was like a firework going off. That bit at the start, the fizz, and then he saw a steady rocket heading up to the sky. Franco turned around just in time to see the light missile hit the back of the boat. It had hit the water early, but what it did was cause enough of an eruption that the rear end of the boat collapsed and water started flooding in. Quickly, the little boat became submerged, and Franco jumped off the side and swam directly to the Isla Juncal.

He was in real trouble now. His mind raced. They had a boat, but if he could get to the island, they couldn't berth, could they? On the island, he might even hide. Where? Where could you hide on an island like this? After all, it was flooding.

He tried to calm himself. Tried to remember to put in powerful strokes, not simply splash around. *Come on, Franco*, he thought. *Come on!* He could hear the boat behind him, but clearly, it was getting too close to the submerged island as the engine was cut. Ahead of him, he could see little bits sticking up, and a flash of moonlight showed him he was heading for the middle of the island.

Gradually, he felt like there was less water below, and he could put his feet down. He quickly pulled through the vegetation and emerged from the water, though his feet stayed submerged. The trees around him and the loose vegetation made it heavy going, and walking was slow.

Desperately, he looked back and he could see a light inflatable. With the engine whirring in the night, it would come close, a flatter hull than any of the fishing boats. They could come right in on that, hunt him down.

He turned and walked as hard as he could, for he couldn't run in this watery mash. If he could get to the other side, maybe he could swim and maybe he would see a fishing boat. There were white lights out there. Single white lights that he could aim for. If he could get on one of them, would they still come for him? Would they kill him in front of other people? Who was he kidding? Of course they would.

There was a splash in the dark. It came from the left. Instinctively, Franco moved to the right, but then there was a splash from the right as well. *Was there one behind? How many?*

Franco never got to finish his thoughts. As bullets ripped into him from silenced guns, he tumbled backwards, writhing, but only briefly, before becoming still. The tide was still rising as his pursuers left him, the only corpse on the Isla Juncal.

* * *

Lobo Silva liked to fish at night. It was quiet, less of the chaos. He could also feel the water bobbing around, even on a reasonably calm stretch, such as he was on now. It was coming close to four or five in the morning, and he was passing by the north side of the Island Juncal.

It had been a decent night's fishing, but fishing these days didn't bring in the money that he needed. The payment from the other people, the British, was worth it despite the risks.

The money had allowed him to buy a car, improve the house, and Juanita would need that.

She didn't stay with him for his looks. If he was lucky, she might have liked his humour. Possibly she even liked the way he cooked, but mostly she liked the comfort she enjoyed from being with him. She enjoyed not being out on the street.

Lobo thought that the night was just about done. He'd taken on board almost three-quarters of the fish he wanted, but with his other work, the amount of fish wasn't that important. He spun the boat round, heading for the Uruguayan side of the tidal inlet, and to the small port which lay beside his home. That was a laugh. A couple of jetties. It wasn't like the bigger ports you saw when fishing further afield off the coastlines to the north of Uruguay or the south of Argentina. But it was home, and it would do.

Something caught his corner of his eye, floating past in the sea. Had it been? Had that been a person? He spun the boat around, quickly manoeuvring back to where he'd been. Of course, the river moved. The body wouldn't be in the same spot, and now the tide was retreating. The water wasn't particularly choppy, and so he was reasonably confident that whatever he saw would be in the same area.

Lobo looked around. He was a vigorous man, built well, and the years of hauling fish had kept his muscles toned and his ability to combat fatigue at a high level. He cruised back and forward over the same spot three times before he saw the figure again.

There was a body. He pulled alongside before carefully reaching down from his little boat to pull the figure onto his deck. The man rolled facedown. Lobo wondered who he was. He was dressed in a shirt which was clearly soaked through from the river. There were trousers and plimsolls. He looked like a man of the city, not from here. He turned him over and then almost started backwards. That was him, the one that the British had shown him.

Chapter 02

Kirsten Stewart stood in front of the coffee machine at a medical facility on the edge of Inverness. It was little known because it dealt with people who had gone off the rails in a rather bad way. She never thought she would see someone she knew in here, but here Craig was. He had his legs blown off below the knee because of a half-botched rescue operation. He had escaped with his life, but Kirsten now thought that he would have been better dead. It would have been better for her, for all she got from him now was anger.

Craig had been an agent like herself, working for the country. As an operator, he was first class. In fact, he'd saved her life on occasion. They had fallen for each other, got together and had many a good time. In fact, they'd left the service to spend time together, only for past enemies to hunt them down and then for Craig to suffer his horrible injuries.

There was one man to blame for that, wasn't there? Godfrey, the head of the service. Kirsten had to make her peace with that. She was going to be working for Godfrey, on an ad hoc basis, taking whatever she could, whatever she felt comfortable with, for she needed money.

It wasn't easy for someone in her position to just roll back into her working past. She couldn't pick up the phone to her former inspector, Macleod, and tell him, 'Oh, I'm coming back.' Not with what she'd done. She had saved the country quite a few times, but she had also learned how to kill. The truth was, she had changed beyond all recognition from the person he had sent to the service.

She took the coffee but almost spat it straight out. The machine looked old, not one of the modern ones that made that rather bland coffee, albeit one that took time. One where they ground the beans for you, doing the job of a barista with all the lack of skill and the lack of feel. Blandness crept in everywhere, she thought.

Having poured half of the coffee away, she walked back down the corridor to see Craig in his end room. Looking through the window, she saw him glance up and scowl. He said something. She didn't know what, but she got the gist amongst the swearing. 'Go away,' was the message, although delivered with a much stronger expletive.

There was a tap on her shoulder, and she turned to see a friendly face. Craig's doctor looked at her wearily, feeling her pain.

'It's going to be a long road and there are no guarantees,' he said. 'We're doing what we can, but he has to learn to accept. He has to learn that . . .'

'What we do,' she said, aware that the doctor knew that Craig had come from the service, albeit not exactly what he'd done, 'sometimes doesn't leave that option open.'

'I thought people like yourselves could adapt. I thought you were trained for that.'

'Adapt to situations on the fly,' said Kirsten, 'but, Doctor, this is different. When you've been that good, when you've been that fast, when you've been able to climb up to the top of the mountain, to have it then taken away from you, . . . I don't know if I would cope. At best, he's going to have a desk job. He never was a desk man. He was a field operator.'

She stopped there, worried she might say too much. The doctor gave a nod of understanding, but he also looked rather bleakly through the window towards Craig. Kirsten turned; two fingers were being held up to her. She was being told to go away again.

'He never swore much before all this,' she said. 'He was quite the gent.'

'I am sorry,' said the doctor, 'but I didn't come here to update you. I came because somebody is waiting for you.'

'Waiting for me?' queried Kirsten, raising her eyebrows. 'Who?'

'I'm afraid I don't always get told the names of the people that arrive in this facility, but he's quite important.'

Kirsten's heart sank. She could do without any other hassles. All she wanted to do was go home, wrap herself up in a blanket and cry. She was losing Craig, really losing him, and there didn't seem to be anything she could do to stop it.

'If you come this way,' said the doctor, 'I'm sorry to rush you, but he said his time was short.'

'Did he now?' said Kirsten. It was better than standing there with Craig, anyway. She couldn't handle looking through that window, remembering the abuse she'd got earlier on her visit. He used to adore her. She used to be a light in his life, but now she seemed to be the figure to hate. Why? She'd gone to rescue him. She'd done everything to get him back. It had just gone wrong. If Justin hadn't . . .

She stopped herself. If Justin hadn't fired that missile which sent the boat they were taking Craig on into the air, they would have disappeared with Craig. He would be in Russia, tortured, ripped apart. Justin did the right thing in trying to stop the boat.

The doctor pointed to a door, punched in some numbers, and pushed it ajar. 'He's in there. Obviously, take as long as you need. If you want me afterwards, ask at reception. They'll put a call out for me, but there's not a lot more I can tell you. Your prognosis is probably more accurate than mine.'

She put out her hand to the Doctor.

'Thank you, Doc. Thanks for all you do here. I may be gone for some time. Take care of him.'

'We will,' said the doctor.

Kirsten walked through the door and saw a man sitting on a medical bed. The room was used for minor treatment. Kirsten closed the door behind her before turning to face someone she didn't really want to see.

'Godfrey, now what can I do for you?' she said.

'Ah, Ms Stewart, tragic, absolutely tragic what's going on with Craig. I see he's getting the best of . . .'

'Don't. We don't talk about him here. I assume you're here because you need me to do a job. You need me to do a job, fine. Talk business. Do not talk about Craig. I still blame you for him being in there.'

'I can see how you would jump to that conclusion,' said Godfrey. 'It's a rather narrow and short-sighted vision, but you haven't been up at my level, so I'll let it slide.'

Let it slide, thought Kirsten. *I'll gut him. If he keeps this up, I'll gut him.*

'But you're right,' said Godfrey, 'it is time to talk business. Have you ever been to Argentina?'

'No,' said Kirsten. 'Why?'

'We've got a job in South America. Franco Manfrin was working for us in Buenos Aires. You see, we've had some trouble there. We believe that there are secrets coming out of South America. Secrets from the organisation. Detailed secrets. Things that people could use. Have you ever heard of Goldsmith?'

'No,' said Kirsten.

'Pity. That's all I've got, the name. That and a dead body operating out of the embassy in Buenos Aires. Franco Manfrin was dispatched to see what he could find. Now, I know information running has been going on. I know that there has been the possibility of people trafficking down there. From Franco's first report, I knew he was getting in with someone, but we weren't sure who. He was due to report soon, but he won't be making a report.'

'Why is that?' asked Kirsten.

'Well,' said Godfrey, 'he seems to have ended up in a tidal inlet between Argentina and Uruguay, picked up by one of my agents.'

'Dead?'

'Yes,' said Godfrey, 'dead. Shot many times. The thing was, he was operating in Buenos Aires, and he ended up crossing the Argentinian border onto an island called Isla Juncal. You probably don't know it, but it's very close to the Uruguayan border. Our operatives in Montevideo were bemused by it. One of our people found him floating in the river, north of the Isla Juncal; he'd been shot many times. If he was on the run back to Uruguay, which is my assumption, he must have either been discovered or he found something that was so big it needed to come in quickly.

'My problem is that there wasn't much found on him, certainly no obvious secrets. I require someone to operate discreetly. They may need to operate over in Argentina as well, continue to Buenos Aires, find out what Franco knew.'

'That all seems a little vague,' said Kirsten. 'When you say secrets coming out, how do you mean?'

'We've got a problem with security there. Checks have been done, and we've looked at those working for us, even put them under interrogation, but we cannot find anything. We believe that there're secrets about people's movements being passed. People who matter. Prime Ministers, royalty, cabinet ministers, people like that being compromised, but it may be more than that. I don't know,' he said.

Kirsten looked at Godfrey and thought she saw worry in his eyes for the first time. He was normally so smooth, so calm.

'Anna Hunt not available?'

Anna Hunt had been Kirsten's initial handler within the service. While she struggled at times with Anna's allegiances, she had a lot of respect for the woman.

'I need someone who doesn't work for us. I need someone who we can deny plausibly, who isn't with us anymore. You left under a cloud. Your boyfriend is in there with no legs, to put it bluntly. You have every reason to hate me, every reason not to work with me. You're being there probably won't be tied to us.'

'Probably?'

'I'm not the only clever bastard in this secret world,' said Godfrey. 'They send them to our universities, to our colleges. There's a reason for that.'

He was always so smug, thought Kirsten. She'd gone to a college, but not a college anybody would recognise the name of.

'I'm worried that something bigger is afoot,' said Godfrey. 'I want you to fly to Uruguay, rendezvous with the embassy there. They'll set you up with the contacts we have, and from that, I want you to track down Franco's movements and contacts in Argentina. I want to know what's going on.'

'My budget?'

'Whatever you need.'

'Am I authorised to kill?'

'You're operating outside of me, but you won't get any complaints from me if you put bullets in anyone.'

'If I find what's going on, do you want me to shut it down, or just report it?'

'Report it in the first instance,' said Godfrey. 'I'll give you an order to shut it.'

'A request, remember?'

'An instruction,' said Godfrey. 'As an employer should do to an employee. I've taken the liberty,' he said, 'of placing some money in your bank account. It'll see you through for a while. Be very careful out there, though. You haven't worked that far from home before.'

'I worked on my own in Alaska,' she said.

'Indeed, you did, and that's why I'm giving you this job, but this is different. Unlike when you're working in the UK, we don't have the same sort of cover. We've got to be very careful about what we do, and how we do it. If you get in trouble in Argentina, we haven't got people to come and get you. Remember, you're always expendable.'

'As if I could forget that,' said Kirsten 'When do I leave?'

'I've booked you on the flight tomorrow from Heathrow. You can fly out of Inverness in the morning. You should be in

Uruguay the next day.'

'Deal,' said Kirsten, much to the surprise of Godfrey. 'Well, I've got to say yes. But understand, you don't just come here and tell me what I'm doing. Just because you stuck money in my bank account doesn't mean I'll always accept it.'

'Of course you'll accept it,' said Godfrey. 'You stand out there and you hate what you see. It's easier to be away from home at the moment, and it's a good reason. National security, bringing the money in, but you are always going to do it. At the moment, the last place you want to be is here. The last thing you want to do is talk to that man in that room. Have a pleasant flight,' said Godfrey, standing up. He walked past Kirsten with a smile, opened the door, and then shut it behind him, leaving her standing, livid with him.

He was right. Godfrey was right, as was so often the case.

Looks like I better pack something light. I'm sure Argentina and Uruguay can be hot, she thought. She turned, walked out of the room and went to look in the window of Craig's room but decided not to. The last thing she needed was another coarse go-away sign to remember him by.

Chapter 03

Kirsten was travelling with one small rucksack which she carried on board the flight out of Inverness. A few hours later, she was on her way to Montevideo, trying to read up about Uruguay and Argentina. It unnerved her a little that she was going to a country she knew so little about, but she was expecting a full briefing at the embassy. Her life had never taken her that way; in fact, it had never taken her out of Europe until she recently went to Alaska.

She mused on how she had changed. Kirsten used to be a simple person. She had enjoyed the basic pleasures of life, spending time with her brother and then spending time with Craig. She remembered the old days of when she'd been a detective working for Macleod and the joy of coming together as a team.

The teamwork was what Kirsten missed; even with Anna Hunt, she'd found a team, but now with Godfrey, she was working on her own. She wanted to get back to a team. Her own team that had operated out of Inverness was defunct. Then Craig had come along. He'd been her team, and they'd made a good pair until Zante.

Kirsten did her usual check of walking up and down the

plane, looking out for anything suspicious. It was a habit that had become a part of her life, looking over her shoulder, checking to make sure nobody was eyeing her, or worse, coming for her.

Having contacted Godfrey that morning, she had asked for some weapons to be made available to her at the embassy. She didn't like the idea of going to a foreign country and especially when Godfrey had said that he wasn't averse to her dispatching anyone. That usually meant that there would be opposition—significant opposition.

One of the disappointing features of operating this way was that she didn't get time to take in the scenery. She'd never been to South America and she quite fancied seeing it. But her days of being a tourist were over. She should have gone around the world in her youth.

After landing at Carrasco Airport in Montevideo, Kirsten cleared arrivals and spotted a man in the dark suit and sunglasses. He held up a board that read, 'Anderson Products' and she walked over to shake his hand.

'My name's Tommy,' he said, in a strong Newcastle accent. 'It's a pleasure to welcome you, Miss Stewart. I do hope that you'll enjoy your stay with us and that we can accommodate you in any way you require.'

'Thank you, Tommy. It's Kirsten though.'

As she shook hands, Kirsten looked across at the far side of the arrivals' hall. There was another man with a board, but he didn't seem to have anyone approaching him. He was older, with a bald head, but he seemed confident. Yet his eyes were everywhere but not looking. It was a telltale sign. When you're waiting with those boards, you have one of two aspects. You're that guy who just doesn't care whether your client arrives, or you're the one who's actively looking for them. This guy was actively looking back at Kirsten all the time.

'I think we should get to the embassy, Tommy. I have some paperwork to catch up on.'

'Of course,' said Tommy, reaching down and taking Kirsten's small rucksack. 'Have you brought anything else?'

'No, I think most of my items have come separately,' said Kirsten.

The ride to the embassy was quiet, and Kirsten didn't look around her, preferring instead to focus on the job at hand. Tommy said nothing from the front seat.

The car pulled round the back of the embassy, Kirsten arriving via the servant's entrance, but she was quickly taken to Ambassador Susan Dandridge. She was a tall and elegant woman heading towards her late fifties, but she carried the role well. Shaking Kirsten buy the hand, the Ambassador ordered some coffee before sitting behind her large desk. She offered Kirsten the seat in front of it, and the two of them waited until the coffee had been served and the door of the room closed.

'Welcome to Montevideo,' said the Ambassador, 'but I doubt you'll be staying long with us; most of the action's on the Argentine side. I have a small package for you,' and she pointed to the cardboard box on the corner of her desk. Kirsten reached for it, opened it up, and saw two handguns inside, complete with ammunition.

'I take it they're satisfactory,' said the Ambassador.

'Absolutely. What can you tell me about Franco Manfrin?' asked Kirsten.

'Well, Franco was picked up by one of our agents in Buenos Aires, recruited to work for us. We're getting a lot of heat at the moment, with secrets moving out of Argentina. We know this because we've put out some red herrings. The trouble is that they seem to be onto our red herrings as well. That's bad enough, but we believe it's a British citizen that's doing it, and we need you to find out who and why. A lot of things that seem to go missing are about movements of very, very important people. They also seem to be about what they're doing in Britain.'

'But they're coming out of the Argentine office,' said Kirsten. 'How's that work?'

'Exactly, somebody's gaining access through Argentina. I'm not sure how—that's what Franco was to look into, but now Franco's dead, so you'll have to look into that.'

'Do you have any idea how this is happening, then?'

'Well, Franco had the idea that communication was being run from Argentina into Uruguay, crossing the river outlet near the Isla Juncal. He may have been right with that, but we've not been able to substantiate it. I've got an operative, Lobo Silva, watching the fishing community near the border. He's a fisherman himself, has lived around here for a long time, and he's struggling to see what's going on. Start with him; he also found the dead man in the water north of the Isla Juncal. I suspect Franco was made. We never received a signal from him, but again, that's not uncommon if he had to run. It looks like he possibly was coming from the Argentine side, over to the Uruguayan side.'

The Ambassador threw a map down on her desk and Kirsten stood up to look at it. 'That,' said the Ambassador, pointing to the map, 'is the Isla Juncal. Franco was found just north of it. When the tide comes up, depending on how strong the tide is, it will flood, sometimes completely. There's no reason to be on that Isla. Why Franco would be there, except for escaping,

I have no idea. Unless somebody took his body to dump, but why there? If they'd found him out, he'd have been executed in Buenos Aires. It's a long way to come to dump a body, and especially one that then gets found. You'd just bury him.'

'Was there anything on him?' asked Kirsten.

'Well, Lobo searched him before he handed him to the police. The only thing on him was a wine list from a club in Buenos Aires—El pájaro raro. That seems a little strange. If he was on the run, the last thing he would have wanted was to be tied to Buenos Aires, so he would have ditched that wine list. But he still had it on him.'

'Do I get to meet the local station officer?' asked Kirsten.

'I'm afraid not,' said the Ambassador. 'I believe Godfrey wants this run so that you are completely separate. So, you'll be talking to me, obviously on the cover that you're doing your work. Then, if anything untoward happens, we can deny you. Sorry about that.' The Ambassador gave a faint smile.

'Don't worry,' said Kirsten. 'I'm used to the idea that nobody wants me at the moment.'

'We can furnish you with whatever you need,' said the Ambassador, 'and you're welcome to operate quietly out of a room here. Although if we want to maintain the idea of you being here for work or travel, it's probably best that you take up lodging somewhere else.'

Kirsten looked down at the map. 'Lobo Silva,' she said, 'where does he operate out of?'

The Ambassador pointed to an almost indistinguishable mark just across from the Isla Juncal.

'Where's that?' asked Kirsten.

'That's a small town where Lobo has always lived. He's ideal as a spy because nobody in the local area suspects him.

His fishing has gone well, but the extra money he earns has not made him daft. He's able to attribute it to family that have passed on. Of course, it's coming from us. He's not ostentatious, though, hasn't upgraded his boat. He's been a very good boy regarding being an operative, so please don't go heavy-handed with him.'

'Is that a hotel resort? Just down from where he lives.'

'Yes,' said the Ambassador, 'it's quite classy, actually.'

'Then that's where I'll book in. I'll work out of there. Bad idea if I work out of the embassy; I bring a lot of heat. I noticed someone at the airport already.'

'Really? Tommy didn't say.'

'No, Tommy didn't see,' said Kirsten. 'Don't have a go, though, disguise was good. I'm just used to being tailed. You pick up on it.'

Kirsten sat for a moment, thinking things through. 'I'll hire a car,' she said. 'I'll do that on my own, but I'll get it brought to the embassy so I can depart in a couple of hours. Just so I know what's going on, I'll need a thorough briefing on the local area and a get-in plan if I'm going over to Buenos Aires. We'll see how things develop. How long would you say these secrets have been passed?'

'At least three months.'

'Is there anything that indicates a finality, anything that points towards some completion of a plan? Is there anything in the secrets that are being passed that you think are pointing towards one thing?'

'No,' said the Ambassador. 'We believe, as I said, that it's movements about very important people, but it just seems so widespread.'

'But they could be potential targets?'

'That's my theory, that they're looking for a target. But the information at the moment is quite basic, or at least what we've intercepted.'

'And how have you done that?'

'We caught a couple of people on the move, but they looked like they were bottom of the scale. They've told us who they were transporting. They know some of the information that's been given because they were told to pass it on if anything happened, but it's very low level. It's basically, "So-and-so will be here at this time. They're on a trip to here; they're on a trip to there," but it's the stuff that the public don't know. In fact, you'd have to be fairly high up to know it. I certainly wouldn't know it—no need to know it.'

'Give me a look at that wine list,' said Kirsten. The Ambassador produced a photocopy and placed it in front of Kirsten. 'Any markings on it?' she asked.

'No. Checked for fingerprints, though, and they're his, a few other people's, but it's a wine list, and there's nobody who came up in our register.'

'Okay,' said Kirsten, 'I think I've got all I need. I think I need to book into the hotel. I'll go downstairs. If you can give me one of your locals who I can talk to, and then I'll depart.'

She took the weapons and placed them in her rucksack. After throwing it on her back, she reached over and shook the hand of the Ambassador.

'I'll be in touch,' said Kirsten, 'but may not be through conventional methods. Be on the lookout. No fall-back plans,' she said. 'If you want to disown me, then this needs to be the only meeting we've had.'

'That's understood,' said the Ambassador.

'Is there anybody else down, though?' asked Kirsten suddenly as she went to leave the room.

'What do you mean?' asked the Ambassador.

'Anybody else down from the office, Godfrey's office?'

'No,' she said, 'are you expecting someone?'

'This is quite serious if he's asked me to come in. We're running an operation in Argentina, so why bring me in? Why not sort that in-house? He's told me we're having problems. That makes me think it's very serious. I was wondering if he would drop Anna Hunt down.'

'Don't know the name,' said the Ambassador.

'Justin Chivers?'

'I saw Chivers three years ago; it was before he got moved up to Scotland.'

'His boss is Anna Hunt—at least she was.'

'I don't know her,' said the Ambassador. 'I'm here to help you and I won't lie to you about what we've got going on. You're in to do a job and the reason it's you is that you're disposable. If it all goes wrong, we can deny all knowledge. That's why you're in. Godfrey said that's the sort of person he wanted to hire, and he said you were the right person for the job. I take it you are.'

'Very much so,' said Kirsten. 'I'm the right person, but I've been in this game long enough to always check I'm not being played.'

'Not by me,' said the Ambassador. 'If they're running secrets out through here, it looks bad on me. I'll be quite happy if you tidy everything up.'

'Well, thank you,' said Kirsten. She gave a nod and opened the door to suddenly be accompanied by a man in uniform.

'John, if you'll take Miss Stewart downstairs; she's asking to speak to one of our local guides for information about the area.'

'Of course,' said John, and he pointed down the stairs. *Well, here goes*, thought Kirsten. *I'd better listen well to the local briefing.*

Chapter 04

Kirsten spent three hours in a briefing with one of the locals at the British Embassy before she hired a car and drove to the resort and spa across from Isla Juncal. The resort was quite splendid—'Five star,' they would say, although she didn't know how they rated things in Uruguay. She asked the Ambassador to contact Lobo Silva, and for his photograph. Kirsten asked her to arrange a meet on the beach by the hotel the next day, around about nine o'clock in the morning.

For the rest of the evening, Kirsten drove directly to the hotel, got her room, and then sat in the restaurant enjoying a light meal. Her shoulders were sore, and she was aching after the flight, but part of her felt good. She was back doing what she was good at and there was a puzzle on her mind other than that of Craig.

Maybe it wasn't great to say it, but she like the danger, and she'd become dispassionate enough to kill the bad guys at least. She'd have to be careful, though; she was out on foreign soil. Uruguay wasn't particularly unfriendly, but Argentina was an old British enemy. She certainly wouldn't want to get too heavy-handed. Kirsten doubted they would take kindly to a British spy on their shores.

As she started dinner that night, she spotted the man from the airport, the bald-headed one who had stood with a sign awaiting someone who never came. He kept glancing over at her, and she wondered why. He gave the impression he was attracted to her. She was dressed in a light T-shirt and flannel trousers, hardly any sort of beauty on the far side of the room. He also seemed to have a wife with him, but he was paying her next to no attention. He looked across at Kirsten frequently. When she caught him looking, he gave a smile, as if he was interested in pursuing a conversation.

Kirsten wasn't interested in him, and she continued at her table, sipping on a small glass of wine after she had finished her dinner. She stepped out of the hotel that night, looking at the Isla Juncal. The tidal passage was not flooded, and the island looked quite large. She found it difficult to imagine all the shrubbery suddenly disappearing under the sea. Argentinian shores could be seen across the passage beyond the Isla.

Franco Manfrin had come from there. He had tried to get across, and for some reason, he'd been on the Isla Juncal. Why? Would you swim from the other side? Not that far, but it was far enough. Swimming was a poor form of escape. You were slow, and anybody in a boat or other watercraft could easily catch you.

As the sun descended, Kirsten took her leave and went back to her room, checking it for bugs. When she was happy there were none, she locked the door, but she slept with her guns under her pillow. The night was warm. She lay only in a light T-shirt.

In Scotland, the house was always warm, the bedroom also at night, but this was a different heat, more suffocating. The air conditioning in the room didn't seem to do much, and she

27

had left it off. Kirsten preferred to hear everything around her rather than that noisy contraption whirring away in the background.

The following morning was bright, and Kirsten made her way down to the gym of the hotel. She ran five miles on the treadmill, finished, and thought about going into a boxing workout as she stood sweating from her exertions.

She noticed the bald-headed man again. Was he something, or was he just a perv? He certainly wasn't embarrassed about looking. Kirsten went to her room, and after showering, put on a light skirt and top and stepped out onto the beach at the far side of the hotel. She had to cross the road to do it, but soon, she was walking along the sand, although it felt different to the sand of home. Back in Scotland, there were many beaches of pebbles, but there were some that were pure sand, and they felt great between your feet. This one, however, seemed coarser. Maybe it was more of a soil, more silt than sand.

As she stood with a light wind blowing across her, she saw a man at the far end of the beach. He wore three-quarter-length jeans and a shirt but had shoulders that looked like you could put bricks on them. He was reasonably young, maybe in his early thirties, and had that tanned complexion that South Americans have, contrasting with her own pale skin. Scotland didn't afford that sort of sunshine and she wouldn't use any beauty products to achieve a tan.

She walked towards him and on approach, recognised the face from the photograph she'd seen in the embassy. Carefully, she turned and walked to the water's edge, standing, looking out at the tidal inlet. He passed by her, then turned and stood a few feet from her, apparently enjoying the view as well.

'Lobo Silva,' she whispered.

'Yes, I take it you're Miss Stewart.'

His English was good, which was a comfort because her Spanish wasn't the best. She could read the language to a degree, but speaking and listening to it was still well beyond her. Since becoming an agent, she'd learned a few languages, but none of them to a point that she felt herself confident in any non-English-speaking country. She certainly wouldn't blend in like a local. Her voice was about as good a disguise as her skin.

'That's the Isla,' he said. 'I was just north of there when I found him.'

'You think he was running?'

'Not anymore,' said Lobo, 'but I think he was hunted—shot several times. They must have used something quiet, as there were plenty of fishermen out there.'

'Did he swim over? Were there any signs of a boat?'

'There's a boat missing from the far side, so I've heard, but whether that's him or whether it just lifted off, who's to say? It's the right place, though, to make the crossing. If he came across, he would have headed for just south of here down to my town. Taxi from there into Montevideo, off to the embassy. Then, whipped out of the country. That's how you do it, isn't it?'

'I don't do extractions,' said Kirsten. 'I do problems, and there's a problem at the moment. What do you know, Lobo?'

'I am here to watch the fishermen, watch the river. There are plenty of boats back and forward, and I have suspicions. Some of them look a little heavier in the water than they should. Whether they're carrying goods or people, who's to say? Sometimes we see people on the other side, people we don't know, but nobody's stopping them. Nobody thinks more than they may be errant fisherman from the other side. I slip back and forward to that border, but I don't land on the other side. I catch my fish and bring to this side. The Argentines generally keep to their side, but most of the fishermen are from here.

'It's the fishermen from here that I worry about. They who seem to have heavier loads coming back. It's difficult because you go out for some good fishing, you take on a large catch, and the boat will go down. But sometimes, the birds don't follow the boats. When you have fish, birds follow.'

'How long have you watched?'

'Over five months. I was doing this before they were worried.'

'Did you notice that back then?'

'Yes, and reported it.'

'What about the wine menu that Franco was carrying?'

'From a place in Buenos Aires. I don't know it as I've never been. I don't go to Argentina. You need your passport. You need to . . . well, with what I know, it's safer for me to be on this side. You never know who knows about you.'

'That's true,' said Kirsten. 'You're a wise man, Lobo.'

'You'd be wise to come out with me on the boat. We can say you're sightseeing. We do that sometimes, take out a tourist. You look like a tourist.'

'Good. I'm staying in the hotel. And I'm meant to look like a tourist. How could I look like I come from here?'

Kirsten kept checking around her, but did so calmly. She turned and held her hands up as if she was staring off into the distance, and then around the other way. Lobo took the hint and totally ignored her, looking off at the boats on the inlet.

'Was there anything on Isla Juncal that you would run for?'

30

'No, I know it was flooding. He was in the water, so if they caught him in Argentina, why dump him in the water and not simply bury him? If they caught him over here, why dump him in the water? He's not a fisherman. Fisherman, yes, dump him, but he was shot. They knew he was shot.

'He probably wasn't shot on this side, and he probably wasn't shot over there then. I think he may have been shot on the Isla. Few people go onto it. They thought that the tide would take him, leave him at the bottom of the sea, sweep him out maybe. But the tide was coming in, lifted him off the Isla and took him north. I caught him before he came back out. You should come out with me. I'll show you those who I have suspicions about.'

'You don't seem to have strong suspicions,' said Kirsten. 'People who are coming back with boats that may be heavy due to fish aren't much evidence.'

'And they spend money. I know about spending money because your government pays me, and I make sure I spend it sensibly so it doesn't look like it comes from them. It's come from a small inheritance or a win on the football. Somewhere else, somewhere that I can account for it. They spend money but they haven't shown where they're getting it.'

'Well, now I am interested,' said Kirsten.

'Well, tonight, come tonight. Meet me at the north end of the beach. I'll take you for a night on the river.'

'I don't get offers like that anymore. See you then.'

Kirsten watched as he walked away to the north end of the beach. He had fantastic shoulders and that figure. Not a model with lots of muscle, but a working man's figure. Genuine subtle muscle, muscle from hard graft, and in truth, he had a pleasant smile with it. She almost cursed herself. She needed to think

31

better of Craig, but she found it hard.

Kirsten returned to the hotel to pick up her bikini and towel before returning to the beach for a spot of sunbathing. There was quite a wind blowing, and she found a sheltered spot from which she could watch the comings and goings out on the water. There was a lot to find out, and she knew she'd have to be careful.

She was there as a tourist, so most of the work would probably get completed at night. She lay out in the shade of a large tree with the sand beneath her. At first, she was restless, but then fell into that quiet watch she had. Kirsten could just about fall asleep, but her senses stayed awake. She wouldn't sleep tonight, so she would need to get what rest she could.

Kirsten returned for dinner that evening dressed in a long skirt and a light blouse on top and heartily ate a steak. Her voyeur was still looking at her from the far side of the restaurant. She tried this time to give him a smile, and he looked back, grinning. His wife was beside him. Clearly, she'd seen what he was doing, but she was not paying him any attention. This raised thoughts in Kirsten's head that the scene wasn't genuine. Who was this man? There were other guests in the hotel, some European, others were American, or from the countries around. But Kirsten kept her thoughts to herself.

When she got up at the end of the night to return to her room, she saw her bald-headed admirer walk across and feign an accidental collision.

'Well, I do say I'm sorry, ma'am.' He was American. It was the first time they had spoken, but she found him placing hands on her arm, steadying her, in an almost too familiar a fashion.

Then she felt a touch on her backside, like he'd had a feel, but Kirsten shrugged it off.

'It's okay,' she said. 'You've had a little too much, have you?'

'Well, never is enough too much. Why don't you come and have a drink with me?'

'I wouldn't want to intrude on your wife.' He looked over.

'You can't intrude on her. She's dead. Dead, I tell you. I look forward to the times on my own. Although, I prefer to share them with someone.'

'Well, I need to get to bed. It's been a long day,' Kirsten said curtly.

'Well, make sure you look me up,' he said. 'We'll talk some more. You are here for a few days?'

'I'm here for a while,' said Kirsten. 'I'll look out for you.'

She had no intentions of doing so, but she wanted to know where he was because she wasn't buying the frustrated husband act. Kirsten walked slowly back to her room, picking up a couple of bottles of water on the way. It was so much warmer here.

She needed to make sure she was hydrated, especially before she went out on the water tonight. There was little time to sit and rest before she'd be back out again, but Kirsten was bothered. Why had he grabbed her like that? He'd come close, inappropriately, grabbing her backside, but it was like a delayed reaction. She took off her skirt and laid it on the bed, then her top as well. Slowly, she ran her hands over them. In the rear pocket of the skirt, a small pocket, almost one you would forget about, she found it. It was a tiny microphone.

Kirsten left it beside her bed and walked around for a bit. She ran the shower, then she made her way back to get changed. Kirsten searched through her phone and found some snoring sounds on the internet. After downloading them, she set them up to play in a continuous loop, placing the phone on the pillow just over from where the microphone was now located. She'd have to be quiet when she left, but at least the man might think she was in the room for the night.

She dressed in black this time, taking her leather jacket to go on top of a black T-shirt and leggings. *It could be cold out on the water*, she thought. She wasn't taking any risks. She jimmied up the window of the hotel and climbed out that way, disappearing off into the dark for a rendezvous at the beach.

Chapter 05

Kirsten waited at the north end of the beach for Lobo to arrive. She didn't hide in the shadows, wanting to make sure she was obvious to him. She could always say she was out on a walk from the hotel if anyone else spotted her. The clouds obscured the moon on what was a dark night, but Kirsten heard Lobo before he arrived. A spy he may be now, but he seemed unaware of how to mask his approach.

'Hello,' he said. 'It's a good night for spying, no?'

'It's a good night for a fishing trip,' said Kirsten, and followed him as the man walked back off the beach. They arrived at Lobo's boat shortly after, and Kirsten jumped on board while Lobo untied the mooring lines, and they set off out into the dark of the sea inlet. The tide was rushing in, and the Isla Juncal was smaller than what Kirsten had observed during the day. Maybe it was the dark of the night though, because the water looked like thick molasses, more of a turgid flow.

Kirsten stood in the wheelhouse at the side of Lobo, finding herself struggling for room. The man was big, broad-shouldered, and although he was trying his best, the wheelhouse wasn't the largest. After half an hour, Lobo dropped the anchor of the boat.

'We'll make out that we're going to rest here, and we'll watch from the rear of the boat. The wheelhouse shows us too much because of its panel lights.'

He led Kirsten to the aft of the vessel, where they both went down on their knees, watching over the edge. There were boats passing this way and that, white lights on top, but Kirsten was amazed at the stillness. Their own vessel was rolling ever so slightly, but it was more like a lullaby than any sort of forced judder on the boat. Lobo handed over a pair of binoculars to Kirsten, took a pair out for himself, and started looking around.

'What about that boat there?' asked Kirsten.

'That's Barbosa. Don't worry about him. Good man. Been here all his life. Not daft, wouldn't get into anything. Nothing unusual about him.'

'That one over there.'

'Too large. It doesn't berth in the jetties this side that will give you easy access to get away quietly. It uses the larger ports. The trouble with the larger ports is there are too many eyes. You need somewhere quiet to run ashore.'

Kirsten sat back and relaxed. The night air was warm, but it was breezy. She was far from home, far from that usual crisp coldness that dominated the Highlands for so much of the year. Even in summer, it wasn't like this. You could still get a cool wind coming through and only on very rare days did you get a warm wind like this. Even then, the humidity was so low, it didn't compare.

She felt herself sweating under her clothing and wondered if she could get used to a life like this. She understood the looser clothing, the desire to stay out of the sun, but even at night she felt uncomfortable.

'I have some water if you want it, or maybe something stronger?' said Lobo.

'I'm on the job,' said Kirsten. 'Water is fine.'

'Over there,' said Lobo, pointing to a vessel. It was the first of many vessels that Lobo pointed out within the next hour, none of whom he had firm evidence on. Yet they were vessels, he thought, at some point or other may have taken someone or something on board. People or goods, vessels that occasionally looked like they shouldn't be so low on the waterline. Kirsten made a note of each of them, but then she saw Lobo's face form a smile.

'Over there,' he said. Kirsten swung the binoculars round until, in the rather poor light, she could just about make out the name of a vessel. *Malvina*.

'Who's that?' she asked.

'The *Malvina* is owned by Pacho Herrera. I have my suspicions about him. He seems to have too much money, much more than others. It's been a steady income as well. Some of them, they're up one month, the next month, they're not showing any money. But him, he's always got money. Too much. New appliances in the house. New car. He doesn't look like a fisherman at all now. The shirts, the clothes, the shoes.'

'Can we watch it?' asked Kirsten. 'Are you able to follow at a distance?'

'If we switch off the light, we can do it. If I keep the light on, he'll see us, and he'll know after a while that we're following him. That's all right if they're going to a particular fishing ground. He may think that we're just chasing a good catch, but if he heads for shore or elsewhere, it will be so obvious.'

'In that case, switch off the light,' said Kirsten. She sat back on her bottom and looked up at Lobo, who was staring down at her.

'What?' she asked.

'When I was a slightly younger man,' he said, 'I used to dream of finding a good-looking woman and bringing her out on my boat for the night. Now finally, I get to do it, and all she wants to do is follow around other boats.' He gave a quiet laugh, and Kirsten smiled.

'It's the glamour of the job,' she said.

Kirsten sat in the aft of the vessel with her binoculars trained on the *Malvina* ahead. In the wheelhouse stood Lobo, and the only lights on the vessel were those of some controls at the helm. Lobo had various cloths up at the window, trying his best to obscure any of the panel lights. Kirsten thought he'd done a good job, but the night was so dark, any random light could give them away. After an hour, Lobo waved Kirsten up to the wheelhouse.

'He's heading into a small harbour,' he said. 'They may put a bit of catch ashore, or they may be up to no good. We don't know where they started from tonight, or indeed, if they've been out for a while. I haven't seen him for the last day or two.'

'I take it that it wouldn't be wise for us to roll into the harbour behind them,' said Kirsten.

'Not unless I'm landing a catch, which I haven't got. I'd also have to switch the light on or maybe pretend it was cracked.'

'No,' said Kirsten, 'that's drawing too much attention. It's also going to highlight you. Your cover is important here. If mine gets blown, I disappear. If yours gets blown, you're at risk. Get close to the harbour they're going into. Somewhere where I can jump ashore. Then stay off until you see me signal you.'

Lobo nodded. 'What do I do if I don't hear from you, though?

How long are you expecting to be?'

'If the *Malvina* has left and you don't see me within an hour, then go home. As long as the *Malvina* is here, though, stay about. Fish if you have to.'

Lobo followed the *Malvina* until he saw it entering the harbour and then routed slightly south along the edge of the tidal inlet. He pulled up close, only a few feet from the edge, in a spot which seemed to be deep enough for a boat as well. Kirsten leapt, landed on the solid ground, and turned and gave a quick thumbs up to him. Then she tore off into the undergrowth.

Kirsten stayed in the darkness, making her way close to a road, but never actually on it. There weren't many cars, for the night was getting old, but when they came, she got down low, hiding herself away.

It took about twenty minutes until she could see the *Malvina*, now tied up alongside. Pacho Herrera and the few crew he had on board were busying themselves about the vessel. They didn't seem to offload anything, and certainly, no one was there to meet them. After watching them for ten minutes, Kirsten skirted round the edges of the harbour to see if there was anyone waiting for contact.

The entire area suffered from a lack of street lighting, for which Kirsten felt blessed. Often back in Scotland, the lighting was good, meaning she had to stay out wider in the shadows, but here, shadows were everywhere. As she got closer to the harbour, she hid behind a parked car, an old beat-up Ford. As she stayed down low, she noticed something in the distance. She took out a small eyepiece that she carried, powerful for its diminutive size, and stayed perfectly still. Watching closely, she thought there was a man standing still in the undergrowth.

When he moved, she could identify the bald head. His figure slowly became apparent to her in what little light there was. Kirsten recognised the man from the hotel. First, he was watching her, now he was watching Pacho Herrera. More than that, he hadn't been out in the water, had he? He knew Pacho was coming here. Could he be the contact?

That idea was blown when Pacho and his crew left the boat and walked inland. She saw the bald man making his way in the shadows behind, and Kirsten followed suit. Being at the end of a tail was always awkward, but she spotted Pacho entering the taverna. The bald man followed shortly.

She would need to get close, for she wanted to know who Pacho was talking to. Had he gone into the bar simply for drinks, or was there another reason?

Slowly, Kirsten crept through the shadows, sticking to the dark patches, not ready to come out. But she realised that if she was going to find out anything in that bar, she'd have to go inside. There were people drinking on some outside seats, but Pacho hadn't come out. Maybe he was seated at the bar.

Slowly she emerged from the darkness, wandering down the centre of the road. It was dusty, small stones underneath her feet, not like the firm pavements of home. Kirsten felt sticky in the humid night air and was glad for the light breeze, even though it was warm. She could feel herself sweating, the clothes clinging to her. A girl from the Highlands, the one thing she didn't like was too much heat. Spain, Portugal, places like that, yes, they were warm, but not like this. This was claustrophobic.

As Kirsten got closer, she saw a man wandering from behind a house towards her. Staggering this way and that, his shirt was half open, and she guessed he must have been in his forties.

He was saying something, presumably in Spanish, but it was so quick that she couldn't understand a word of it. He seemed to slur as he spoke too, making the language even more difficult for her to comprehend. She went around him, not noticeably, but just gently, as if he was just a distraction in the night. But the man moved closer to her. He said something in Spanish and Kirsten gave him a look of confusion.

'Sexy lady,' he blurted.

No, thought Kirsten, *it's the last thing I need*. He then started making some quite grotesque gestures about Kirsten's shape. Highlighting certain characteristics of her body that he seemed to enjoy the most, he grabbed her attention, but she kept half an eye on the taverna. If needs be, she'd brush this guy off physically because she needed to get inside the taverna quickly.

'You come back to my place,' said the man. 'We . . .' and then he started gyrating his hips in a highly sexualized way. *Not likely*, thought Kirsten. *Besides, at the speed you're doing that and the way you're doing it, you'll probably have a hernia before we get too far.*

She half laughed. Her defences were down slightly as she walked past him, but he reached out and grabbed her. Kirsten quickly took a wrist, driving it up round the back of the man, but then she felt a pain. She looked at her shoulder. The man had driven a needle into her.

She glanced back at his face, which she thought gave a rather twisted smile. Kirsten pulled hard on his wrist again, and he cried out, but then her hand slipped off. Stumbling back slightly, her head spun, and the ground heaved this way and that. As she felt her senses reel, she realised she'd been drugged.

41

Chapter 06

The world was spinning. Kirsten could still see the allegedly drunk man in front of her and could even pick out the needle in his left hand. He came towards her, and she lashed out with a kick. She could feel that it connected somewhere with his hip and not up at his hand where she intended, but then again, she was amazed that it even hit at all. Her limbs were doing whatever they wanted, not what she wanted. She tried to focus, and she threw a fist at the man. She wasn't sure how much she missed by, but she definitely missed. He shouted, crying out for help.

Who was he? Had she been watched coming in? Was this part of Pacho Herrera's posse monitoring strangers? Had the bald man spotted her? Whatever, she was in a state of confusion and had no backup to get her out.

Kirsten felt a punch to her face, and she reeled from it, but in some ways, the sharp pain helped. Instinctively, she whipped round a leg from behind her, catching the man somewhere around his head with as strong a kick as she could manage. She heard him hit the ground, but the ground beside her suddenly tipped left and she stumbled that way. Then she stumbled right. Then she looked off into the dark.

They were whispering. So many were whispering. It sounded like a cacophony of cockroaches scuttling here, there, and wherever, but something was in there. Something was in the darkness. She could see limbs, insectoid limbs.

She heard a cry from the taverna and saw men running towards her. Kirsten raced into the darkness of the scrubland, but as she got there, she saw it was alive, seething and rolling. A hundred thousand cockroaches or something like them suddenly covered her legs. She kicked all around her, but she couldn't hit anything, and she spun and fell over.

She looked up from amongst the mass, feeling them crawling across her back, in front of her face, thousands of little legs. More poured over a small landmass towards her. Kirsten rolled this way and that and then tore off again. She found an uprooted tree, and the base of it provided a solid backdrop to hide behind. She knelt down and tried to get herself to focus.

There can't be lots of cockroaches here. There can't be swarms like that. It's not right, she thought. She heard the cries of the men searching for her. Then she heard something else. In the tree above her, something was creeping. A cold sweat ran down Kirsten's neck. She could feel her arms beginning to tremble, her heart skipping a beat. On the left side of her, a long limb descended before another one came across on the right. She rolled her head backward ever so slightly and saw the large fangs that came from a spider's head.

It hadn't seen her. It couldn't see her because it was above her. Did they sniff? Could they detect their prey that way? The spider was huge, each fang almost the size of her head. How did it exist here? When did they get so big?

Stop, she said to herself. *Stop it. It's not real. It's not real. That's from a film. It's from a film.*

43

She looked back up and saw it move ever so slightly. One thing she was sure of, she was sweating profusely, but not from the humidity; this was a cold sweat. This was one of fear. It couldn't be real, could it? It couldn't.

She sat huddled up, unable to move, scared it would attack. She watched as the creature slowly clambered off the tree and onto the ground in front of her. Its abdomen was inches from Kirsten's face. She tried not to breathe. She heard the men in the distance, and then she saw one appearing. The giant spider saw him, and it scuttled over.

Kirsten heard him crying out. First, the spider reared, and then the fangs attacked the victim. She saw the man being wrapped by the spider, crying out desperately for his friends, and then another man came around with a gun. He was searching in the dark, but the spider had gone. It had moved off with its catch, but she saw the man looking towards her hiding spot.

He drifted in front of her slowly, and Kirsten crept up behind him. She would despatch him with quiet, practised ease and then move on. Kirsten had to get away from this place. She had to get away from these creatures, these creatures that weren't real, and yet every sense said that they were there.

She reached up, put an arm around his neck, and went to break it. Then he was gone. Her arm just sailed through where his neck should have been. She flopped down onto her backside, confused. The creature, although she hadn't touched it and it hadn't touched her, had seemed so real. And this man, he was right there, and yet her arm passed through.

There was a hiss behind her. Kirsten turned to see the head of a snake several feet away. The snake was massive; its head, about four times the size of Kirsten's fist. The smart thing would be to move away, but in her current state, she was struggling to think. She lashed out with her fist.

The snake disappeared. *Was any of this real? Where was she?* She had to get out, had to get back to safety. Kirsten had been compromised. *Think! Think!* She remembered the man with the needle, the apparent drunk who had lured her in. *Shoddy*, she thought, *shoddy. Anna Hunt wouldn't like it. Godfrey wouldn't be impressed.*

Stuff Godfrey, she thought. *To hell with it. I've got to get out. Focus. Focus, Kirsten.*

She crawled off in the dark through more scrubland, but she heard a shout. *There were torches now as well, but were there? Were these real people? Was she in trouble or was it just an illusion, something formed by her mind? What had she been injected with?*

She crawled off into another dark corner. This one was a hollowed-out bit of ground, but she could lie flat on her belly. As she lay there, something touched her leg. Kirsten went to kick it, but did that feel different? She saw the spider crawling on her leg. She felt a tingle. Could she just swat it with her hand? She reached down. At the last moment, she thought if she was to do this, she should do it with aplomb, do it with a bit of pace, just in case.

She swiped across with her hand and was startled when the spider was knocked off her. Quickly, she stood and ran. It was real. That one was real. It wasn't a thing of her mind, which then disappeared when she touched it.

Kirsten saw a building on the edge of the roadside and ran towards it. Stopping, she panted, her back up against the building, understanding that she was not functioning as she should have . She needed to be quiet. She needed to just creep away, find the boat, find Lobo, put this all behind her.

Back down the path, she thought. *It'll be back down the path, but could she trust the path? Could she trust anything? She had to react as if everything was real, didn't she?*

You could get this wrong. You could . . . there was a sigh beside her. On the other side of the building was someone. Kirsten trusted her instincts. She waited until feet emerged past the edge of the building and she grabbed the figure before her. He was a tall, powerful man, but she was up and onto him quickly. This time when her arm went around his neck and the hand over the mouth, he felt real. It was only a matter of seconds before she dropped him.

She looked around and saw the road in front of her. Kirsten ran for it as hard as she could, and then instead of a dusty road, she nearly ran into the wall of a house. She'd been on a path, and she had to stop herself quickly before she ran into the side of the building.

Dear God, what was happening? She couldn't trust herself. She couldn't trust anything she was doing. From the corner of the house, halfway up the wall, she saw the long, black leg, spindly yet powerful. Another one joined it, and she saw the fangs emerging around the edge of the building.

Get out, she thought to herself. *Get out of my head.* She stumbled to the left suddenly, unsure if it was the ground that fell or a spasm in her leg that made her drop. She turned her back on the creature, ignoring it. 'It's not real,' she said; 'it's too big. It's not real. It's not something I can believe.'

She looked down at the body in front of her. There were people out there ready to kill her. She peered around the side of the house. A path led out to the road, and she saw a car approaching. It would pass her by shortly.

Kirsten got an idea. She reached around and found a small

stick and crept out along the path towards the road. As the car went past, she flung the stick at it, and she heard the clatter.

That car was real, she thought, *that car is real!*

She stood up and ran as hard as she could. There came a shout, but Kirsten didn't wait for anyone. This was the road. This is the road she came up. Her lungs emptied and twice her left leg seemed to collapse, but she kept herself upright, keep herself moving.

A gunshot whistled past her head. Kirsten had no time to think about what she was doing. She had to get clear, and she had to make sure that whatever else happened, she kept moving back towards the boat. Kirsten recognised the path she was on, realised where she joined the road, and now cut back down where she'd gone before.

As she ran between two trees, she saw a web. On the web were tarantulas. She would have to run through it. Was this real, though? Were there tarantulas out in Uruguay? She didn't know. She needed the guide from the embassy to tell her, to inform her about this place. Kirsten didn't stop, but ran and hit the web. Her breath was held, she was ready for the furry legs to be on her. But they vanished.

She rounded another corner where a man stood with a gun. 'She's here,' he shouted. Instantly, Kirsten threw herself at him, and he vanished, but she collapsed onto the ground.

Not real. Not real, she thought. *His shout wasn't real. I'm good. I'm good.*

She rolled back up, out of breath, but now she could see the bank. She could see the edge of the tidal inlet. There was the boat. There was Lobo, wasn't it?

She ran and as she took off from the edge to jump out onto the boat, it changed into a shark's head. It was bigger than she could ever imagine, its white teeth wide enough to accept her into its mouth.

Don't trust it, she thought as her feet contacted water, but where was the boat? She turned to swim, but where could she swim? She looked back at the land; it had gone. She was in the middle of the ocean. She could see the shark fin circling. *What?*

Her mind raced, and then a hand grabbed her. She felt herself being pulled out of the water, landing on a deck, and she looked up into the face of Lobo. Her hands shot up, and she touched his face, feeling it all over.

'You're real,' she said.

'Yes, I'm real.'

'Get us out of here. Now! Get me back to the hotel. I'm seeing things.'

She saw his smiling face, his nod to say he would do it as quickly as possible. She hoped so, because sitting on the roof of the wheelhouse was the gigantic spider again. Was it smiling at her? It felt like it was smiling. She closed her eyes, but she could still see it.

Chapter 07

Kirsten rolled out of bed and nearly tripped on the clothes on the floor before reaching the bathroom. She threw the lid of the toilet up and vomited profusely into it. She felt grateful that, unlike the previous time when she'd vomited into it, the toilet hadn't bent in shape and turned out instead to be a dragon's head. The surrealism of what she was seeing had diminished.

Taking some water to rinse out her mouth, she flushed the toilet and made her way back to her bed. Lobo, the previous night, had got her to the hotel. However, he couldn't be seen coming in with her. Somehow, she'd got along the corridor despite the enormous spider and the headless pygmy hunter. *What on earth was that about?*

Her dreams had been baffling, but she knew she'd been dreaming. Macleod, appearing in the Widow Twanky outfit at the village hall, told her she was dreaming, as if her former boss would ever get into something like that. She laughed at that one, but overall, she wasn't laughing. *What had she been hit with? Would there be long-term effects?*

She wanted to contact Lobo to find out where they'd been last the previous night and run through what had happened.

She'd been lucky to get away, fortunate to still be in one piece.

She lay on the bed, looking at the ceiling. She reached around underneath the pillow. Where were her guns? Kirsten stood up, realising she had nothing on. She must have come in and just torn off whatever she was wearing. She looked down at the black clothing from the previous night strewn across the floor. There was a gun in there. Kirsten tried to locate a clock. It was eleven a.m. and she stumbled across to the curtains, almost drawing them back before she remembered her current state of attire. Instead, she pulled them slightly to look out, with only her head showing.

The day was sunny. She'd need to make a show. She'd need to be about the resort. If somebody had been drugged the night before, she wanted to make sure that she couldn't be fingered as being that person. She needed water, though. Whatever they'd done to her system, she craved water. She was sweating constantly. Water would be good, though. Flush her system. That was for the best, wasn't it?

Kirsten pulled on her bikini and then covered herself up with a short dressing gown. She exited her room and wobbled her way along to the pool, stopping at the bar and asking for eggs for breakfast. She forced herself to sit there, swallowing them even though every bite seemed to feel like it wanted to come flying back up.

Then she made her way to a sun lounger. Kirsten picked one with an enormous umbrella over the top, so she was lying in the shade. Taking off her gown, she decided she would stay there for most of the day. She looked like a tourist—that was the point. There was nothing for her to do right now. She would get nowhere today, but at least her cover would remain intact.

As she lay there, Kirsten suddenly felt that someone was watching her. She had her eyes closed, but there was breathing close by. She flashed her eyes open and saw the bald man who'd been watching her in the restaurant and who she'd seen last night going to the taverna. He was standing over her, looking down.

'Hello?' he said. 'Can I just tell you that you have a mighty fine body there?'

'Excuse me?' said Kirsten.

'I was just admiring your figure. Forgive me. My name's Charles Hudson. I'm an American film producer and, quite frankly, you're the sort of person we'd like to see on the screen. What's your name, if I may ask?'

He was brazen with it, simply standing there staring, saying it as if he'd paid her some sort of compliment and he was entitled to continue to look her over. Kirsten reached for her water, took a long drink of it, and then lay back again.

'Kirsten Hastings. You're a film producer?' she said. 'What sort of films do you produce?'

'Good ones,' he said, 'and I'd like to offer you an audition.'

'I've done no acting in my life,' said Kirsten. 'You have no idea how I speak; you don't know how I perform in front of a camera.'

'No,' he said, 'but I know how you look and, to be honest, the sort of performing we do is natural.'

Kirsten was ill at ease with his verbal jousting; she wasn't up to it today. Her mind was still reeling. *What was he talking about?*

'I have a studio in Buenos Aires; we've got one here also in Montevideo, and I go back and forward between the two.'

Kirsten's ears pricked up. He was there last night. He's now popping back and forward between Argentina and Uruguay. That's got a cover story that could work. The bald man was worth investigating.

'What sort of films are we talking about?'

'Ones that show off women to their best. We like to feature the women in them more than the men.'

'But like I said, I can't act. I've never done any talking on a stage, on film, anything like that. I don't even know how to learn words.'

'There are few words, and to be honest, people watching our films don't care how you sound. Well, not how you speak.'

A slow realisation dawned on Kirsten, and she found him repugnant. This guy obviously made some sort of pornographic film, and he was standing here gawking at her, asking to make one. In normal circumstances, she'd have told him where to go; she'd have told him what she thought of him. But this was a lead.

'I think I drank too much last night,' said Kirsten, 'but I take it there's good money to be made from this.'

'Someone looking like you, yes,' he said.

'I'll come for an audition,' she said, 'but not now. I need some recovery time; my head's spinning.'

'Well, why don't you join me for dinner tonight?' he said. 'Just you and me and we'll discuss.'

'Are you not bringing your wife with you?'

'No, I'm there to look at you and assess you. I will not need my wife with me, but don't worry. She knows the business I'm in and she's here with me. She's very broad-minded. I'm hoping you're going to be broad-minded as well.'

I'm hoping I'll find things out before I get that far, thought Kirsten.

The man left Kirsten alone, but he passed by several times during the rest of the day. He watched her, occasionally stood in front of her. His eyes cast over her body for almost thirty seconds at a time before he said, 'Beautiful,' and walked off. Kirsten didn't know if she was meant to feel impressed by that, meant to feel special, but she felt like a piece of meat.

Kirsten dressed for dinner, looking elegant in her long skirt and sleeveless top. She wanted to look sexy, wanted to make him think she was interested, that she was the sort of woman who would make herself look good for any man. When she arrived at dinner, he sat beside her, on the same side of a table, and she could feel his hands occasionally moving out to her thighs. He put his arm around her several times while talking to her, and she could see him looking at her, weighing up her body several times. He was gross, but she needed the conversation to keep going.

'Why a studio in Buenos Aires and one in Montevideo? Why not in one place?'

'I see girls from everywhere. I'm hoping to set up more studios. We need to highlight people like you. We need to bring you out into the fore.'

'Do you make English-speaking films?'

'There's not a lot of speaking. We dub over, but like I said, most people aren't that interested in what you're saying. More interested in what you're doing.'

He began talking about money, and Kirsten didn't think the financial remuneration was a lot, considering what she thought he was asking her to do.

'There will, of course, be some men in the film. You get introduced beforehand; it just makes things easier,' he said.

Well, that was something she was going to run away from.

She wouldn't go through with this. After all, she was here to learn about him, not perform for him. Kirsten knew there were people within the spy community who would do that, who would go that far. She envied their lack of scruples, their confidence as well, even if she didn't agree with it.

'Well, what do you think?' he said. 'Would you like to come for an audition?'

'When I feel better,' said Kirsten. 'Not tonight.'

'But come up to the room because I've got some forms I'll need you to fill in.'

Kirsten wondered where the man thought they were at and hoped he wasn't looking for some evening entertainment. She would not be doing that either.

Kirsten rose, and he took her to the lift. She could always feel his hand up her back, then down towards her backside, remembering the mic he had put in previously. She had it with her, as she was in the same skirt. He'd have heard her throwing up earlier if he was listening. He wouldn't have known why, but he'd have heard her. Maybe he'd have heard the racket through the night, but she hoped she hadn't said anything. If she had, this could be dangerous.

The man led the way from the lift to his room, knocking briefly, and Kirsten realised he was in a suite. In the first room sat a young woman talking to the man's wife. The man walked up to his wife, gave her a kiss on the cheek, and then turned to the other woman.

'Well, I'm here now as well, so let's see.'

Kirsten watched uneasily as the woman dropped the evening dress she was wearing and stood there fully naked.

'Yes,' he said, 'you'll certainly do. This way, please.' He turned to Kirsten, pointing towards a bedroom.

'I'd be most grateful if we could do an assessment like that tonight,' the man asked, as if it was the most normal thing in the world. Maybe it was in his world. It wasn't Kirsten's.

'Let's just get the forms,' said Kirsten. 'I'm really not feeling up to it tonight. Wouldn't want you to be disappointed.'

'I doubt I'll be disappointed looking at you,' he said. 'I think you'll knock them for six.' He pointed back out to the woman, who was still standing with nothing on while getting measured up.

'I can provide my sizes without being measured. Is that for fittings?' asked Kirsten.

'No, just some of our watchers like to know the sizes.'

Kirsten's mind reeled. *What on earth?*

'How would you feel about travelling back and forward between Argentina and here? Would you be okay with that?'

'Could be. I'm only here for a while.'

'When you see the money, you might want to stay here longer. This could be a career. This could be a chance for you,' he said. 'Trust me, you've got the natural assets to make your financial assets grow.' He said the word 'assets' like he enjoyed it.

Kirsten always thought she looked good, but she was a fighter. She'd grown up in mixed martial arts and yes, while she thought she looked trim, she never saw herself as overly sexualised. With Craig, it had been different, of course; that side had developed and grown and then died. But he had never been like this man. Hudson was leery, almost pushing you along.

Hudson put out some forms on a table, asking Kirsten to fill them in. There were questions about sexual health. Other questions asked for passport details and about her ability to move freely between countries.

As Kirsten bent over writing it down on the table, the man stood behind her and she could feel his hand running up and down her back. As she finished, he disappeared off to a corner of the room and came back with a small handheld camera. 'If you're up to it, we could do some small shots tonight. I'm just very excited about you,' he said.

I bet, thought Kirsten.

'Can I send initial images of you off to some of our backers?'

Kirsten put a hand up to her mouth and feinted a sick feeling. 'I'm sorry,' she said. 'Better tomorrow. At the moment, I feel like I could throw up. I really overdid it last night. Man, I feel white.'

'Okay,' he said, 'I'll escort you back to your room.'

As they left the bedroom through the front room, Kirsten could see the other woman there, still undressed. When she reached her own room, she found the man was lingering. She opened the door, stepped inside, and he went to step in with her.

'Sorry, I'll have to say goodnight. I think I'm going to . . .' She slammed the door in his face. Because of the microphone, she ran over and pretended to vomit in the toilet and initiated the flush afterwards. She sat down on the bed to think.

Boats going back and forward. Now, some pornographic producer is also travelling backwards and forwards. Is the information flow happening that way? Why was he out last night? Why was he doing it in secret instead of meeting these people with the boats, or was he checking them beforehand? Just making sure they were alone?

Too many questions, thought Kirsten. *Too many questions when I need a good night's sleep.*

Chapter 08

Kirsten awoke the next morning, keen to get out and crack on with the case. She dropped by Hudson's wife, who she saw at breakfast, but she said the man was busy most of the day. Kirsten said she would try to find him later that evening rather than waste another day sitting by the pool. Kirsten contacted the embassy, asking to meet Lobo again. Half an hour later, at the edge of the sandy beach before the hotel, Lobo arrived. He approached, looking wary of her.

'Why in daylight?' he asked.

She walked up to him, put her arms around him, and planted a kiss on his lips. 'We're having a fling. You're going to take me out on your boat. If anybody wonders what we're doing, we kiss.' She took his hand. 'Lead me to the boat, and smile. You've just bagged me.'

'Bagged?'

She saw him give a grin, but underneath, she could feel his tension. She was linking herself to him now, putting him in a position he probably thought was risky, exposing him to undue scrutiny. Kirsten disagreed. It looked now like he was being played by her. That was a better cover, surely.

As they arrived at the jetty holding Lobo's vessel, she hugged him in front of the other fishermen that were about. They stepped inside the boat, and she kissed him, before peeling off her t-shirt and sitting in a bikini top and a pair of shorts. She saw some shakes of the head, some laughs, and she whispered to him he should turn and bask in the shock, give the idea that this is a sudden thing. Lobo did so, and soon they were motoring out into the tidal inlet. They headed south of the Isla Juncal, up the west coast of it, and then steered north.

'Pacho Herrera. I want to see where he is.'

'He was sailing north this morning up the river. I thought that's where you'd want to go. Unfinished business from the other night,' said Lobo.

'I need to know what he was doing. I need to know who he was talking to. He was being followed by an American. I need to know if the American's involved or the American is the main runner.' She told Lobo about Charles Hudson's movie exploits.

'How far do you go with that?' he asked suddenly.

Kirsten looked up at him. 'Not that far,' she said.

'Good,' said Lobo. 'I sometimes wonder about spies. Are you all just morally bankrupt? Do you have nothing there? Sell your souls and your bodies to figure stuff out?'

Kirsten thought about it for a moment. Had she sold her body? No. Never. That she was sure of, and she never would. She had too much self-respect. She knew some spies who had, who delighted in working honey traps, but not her. What about her own morals? What about where she'd . . .

It used to be that she was working for her country and her country's interests, and she justified it that way. Now she was working for money, a mercenary.

'It'll change you,' she said to Lobo. 'You're taking the money now, but you may go further. It'll change you or kill you.'

He gave a grim nod and continued up the river. Kirsten saw several boats about to pass her by and stood up in the wheelhouse, wrapping her arms around Lobo. 'Kiss me,' she said, and together, as the boats passed, they kissed deeply.

'See,' she said. 'It has some benefits.'

'That means absolutely nothing,' said Lobo dryly.

She hadn't realised he was such a romantic. It took two hours before Lobo spotted Pacho Herrera's vessel moored further upriver. There was no one about it. The nearest bank was also quiet. Kirsten pulled off her shorts.

'I'll be back shortly,' she said.

She told Lobo to stay well off the other vessel and dived into the water, swimming up close to Herrera's boat. As she reached it, she could grab the edge of the boat and haul herself on board before lying down low. Once she was certain there was no one else about, she walked into the larger wheelhouse, the boat being almost three times the size of Lobo's.

The wheelhouse was well laid out. There was a chart table, many navigation devices and screens, all switched on but quiet. She heard the occasional chatter from the radio. Again, switched on. It made her wonder what was going on. After all, there was nobody on the vessel. *Wouldn't you have killed the radio, saved the battery?* She searched in the hold, but there was nothing.

Where is the crew? she thought. *Where're the goons?*

She looked at the aft of the vessel. There was no small boat attached, no little rubber dinghy that you could use to get ashore from here. Maybe they had taken it ashore. Maybe they'd gone somewhere, but she thought it strange not to leave someone behind. Part of her felt this could be a trap.

They'd encountered her—at least they'd encountered someone. Would they recognise the woman in black they jabbed with a needle? Well, he'd got a good look at her, the apparent drunk, and although she clocked him, she hadn't killed him. There was only the one man by the house that she had killed. She tried to think out that night, but because of the drugs they had put into her, her memories were hazy.

Kirsten, having searched the holds of the boat, went back to the wheelhouse and started picking through all the papers that were there. There were paper charts and maps stowed up on the side, and she took those out as well, poring over them. The notes were in Spanish, and although she read them, the handwriting was poor. Everything written in another language was simply harder to comprehend. It just didn't come naturally. Everything was forced, and she still felt jaded from being drugged.

Really, she should've taken herself back to the embassy, get a doctor to check her over and make sure she was still okay, but she didn't want to be seen near it.

Kirsten traced her finger along, looking at routes that went from the Argentinian side of the inlet over to the Uruguayan side. Lots of them went round the Isla Juncal, but there was nothing concrete here. They were just routes. There were also other fishing routes running up and down. Locations were marked all along the side, both the Argentinian side and the Uruguayan side. But they were just places where you could stop, places where you could land a catch or go ashore. Just places.

There was no detail on the charts. Nothing said anything illegal was being done. Kirsten felt frustrated. She looked out from the boat and saw that Lobo was quite a distance away now, and she thought it was nearly time for her to return. She gave a signal from the boat, aiming to wave him back towards her, but he wasn't moving. The vessel seemed to be drifting off.

Kirsten wondered what to do. She could swim to it now and she'd reach it. It wasn't that far away. Or if she waited, and it kept drifting, why was it drifting? What was up? Had he just not seen the signal? Or had something worse happened? Because if it had, it had been done quietly.

Kirsten re-entered the water and slowly swam towards Lobo's vessel. There was no one there. From the water, she could see nobody moving. The vessel wasn't that big. Lobo should have been there in the wheelhouse, at least in the back. Even if he was sitting down, she would see him.

Kirsten swam closer, because there were no other boats around, no one else to stop her, no one else interfering. If something had happened, they'd be gone. Long gone. She swam alongside the boat, hauled herself up onto the edge and looked. Lobo was lying face down.

She could see the pool of red coming out from him. Kirsten felt her stomach tense, and she took another chance to look around. Nothing. She'd no gun on her, and the only other thing there were her shorts and top that she'd left after stripping for her swim. She hadn't brought many items with her.

They'd seen her. They'd seen her with him, though. Kirsten reckoned she was at least four to five miles north of her hotel. It was possibly longer, maybe ten. She looked down at Lobo, turned his shoulder slightly, and saw the large slash across the neck. The bastards had left him to suffocate, his throat gagging for air, air that wasn't coming down to his lungs.

He was a big fella, so had they taken them by surprise? Somebody must have come in from the water. You could do it quietly, especially if you were trained to do it. She scanned the surrounding water. No one was coming for her. If this was a setup, they'd have informed the police by now, or were the police on their way? Or maybe they were just having trouble getting a watercraft out here?

She needed to be back in the hotel. They'd been clear of anyone for a while now, so the story would work if she was back on the shore and especially if his boat was missing.

Kirsten looked around and then saw it, a crowbar in the corner. She started hammering away at the bottom of the vessel. Repeatedly, she hit it hard until she saw the first crack, and then she punched it hard again. A hole developed, the water flooding in. She stood back and watched it. The boat would be sunk within twenty, twenty-five minutes.

She grabbed her top, pulled her shorts on, and dived out into the water again, swimming for the edge. When she reached it, she stayed on the banks, heading away in the brush, watching until the boat sank.

'I'm sorry,' she said. 'I said it would kill you.'

Kirsten felt a genuine sorrow. He'd seemed a decent bloke. He'd just been doing his job, and it was unusual in this game to find someone who was not naïve, but so straight with what they were doing. Everyone had their little manoeuvres, had their own ideas of what they wanted. Lobo had seemed to be someone trying to do something decent, taking his pay and doing his job. If the police came to her, she would say he dropped her back. That's if the police even got informed.

That was the other thing. If they were running people back and forth, would they want the police to be involved? Would they want to be indicating that it was them to Kirsten? Did they know who she was? If she was British Intelligence, if she was from the embassy, if she was that type of person and they did this, the heat could come down. If the police got involved, the British would have to work harder. More than that, they might have to work with the Uruguayans who could involve the local police with them.

Sinking the boat was the best, she said to herself as it disappeared from view.

She turned, felling wet suddenly, and ran back towards the hotel. By the time she'd arrived, she was no longer wet with seawater. Dripping with sweat, she snuck in through her own window, and then paraded back out to the hotel pool. Lying there in her bikini, sheltered from the sun, Kirsten wondered what it all meant. She ordered a shot of whiskey and then raised a silent toast to Lobo.

Across from her, she saw Hudson's wife, who smiled, but Charles Hudson didn't appear. Was he involved? Had he set this up? Who had known that she was going with Lobo? Was someone telling him, or had someone just been on patrol around Pacho Herrera's boat and caught them cold? There were too many ideas flowing through her head.

It was daytime when Hudson appeared. Kirsten saw him within the dinner room. She wasn't dressed fancy, but he came over, put a hand on her shoulder, asked if she was feeling better, and she said she was. He said that was good, but he wasn't available for auditions tonight, telling her that sometimes you had to keep the wife happy. Kirsten laughed hollowly and tried to keep from her mind that he may have killed Lobo. Lobo hadn't been romantically involved with her, but she saw herself as a senior agent, and she should have seen it coming.

She did, however, decide that she wanted to watch Charles Hudson and that would start from right now.

Chapter 09

Kirsten sat on her hotel bed, wondering what her next move should be. Someone was onto her, or at least onto Lobo. He'd paid the price for it, and she wondered if they knew she'd been on the other boat. Surely not. Surely, they wouldn't have risked that. There was a list of locations in Spanish that she'd found, but would they have left those there? If they'd known she was going over, would they have left a load of false information, or had they not even been aware she was there?

She'd correctly sunk the boat. That meant his body might not rise for a while. It might stay jammed down there with it. For a moment, guilt came over her. Lobo had been okay until she'd joined him. He was out of the fracas when she'd been stabbed with the needle and had hallucinated, being off the shore in the boat. Had he been seen? Were they stalking his boat that night and just took him out while she was off it? If she'd been there, she might have been able to stop it, or she might have been dead too.

Kirsten would need to report the death of Lobo to the Ambassador to pass back to Godfrey. It wasn't an auspicious start, but it confirmed that something was happening. Something worth killing for. Few people are killed lightly. Most killings happened because someone believed there was no other way around it. That was because, in the spy business, most people were business people. They weren't psychopaths; they weren't people with a taste for blood. Spies were just carrying out business, albeit a deadly business.

It was late, but early enough that the bar of the hotel would still be open. Kirsten dressed in some slacks and jumper and decided to see if Charles Hudson was still about. He was the key to this, and her angst was up at the death of Lobo. Had he been the problem? He'd been there the night before. He was clearly keen on acquiring her for one of his films.

The outside veranda of the hotel linked onto the bar, and she saw Charles Hudson sitting on his own. In front of him was a double shot of what could be bourbon, and she watched as he drank it before ordering another. He was dressed in a jacket, a light shirt, and slacks, and the shoes he was wearing weren't fancy, but this time were dark trainers. Where was he going? The man always looked snappy, but now he almost looked practical.

Rather than join him, Kirsten remained hidden on the far side of the hotel, taking up a seat just out of Hudson's view. Every now and again, she'd lean across, looking past the pillar that was blocking her from him, monitoring the man.

Three bourbons later, he was up on his feet and departing. Kirsten had a weapon with her, hidden away discreetly, and so she followed Hudson, watching him get into a taxi at the front of the hotel. Kirsten scanned some of the cars, saw one with keys in it, and jumped in. There was the option of a taxi, but this seemed easier, and she could also probably have the car back before it was noticed missing the next morning.

As she drove off, she realised the irony of her life now.

She would take cars or motorbikes at random, use them for whatever she needed; before, as a detective, she was totally against the idea and often hunted down people who had taken said cars. She chortled slightly, trying to relieve the tension she felt. The game was deadly. Lobo had paid for it, but she still didn't know what the game was.

The taxi dropped Hudson off at the end of a path by the road. Kirsten drove past before pulling in and parking the car in the shrubbery. By the time she'd raced back to the path, Hudson was walking down it; the taxi had left.

Kirsten stayed in the shadows. As she crept past trees and low-lying plants, she felt a chill, a fear creeping up on her. The night was dark, and the shadows, rotating shades of black, kept giving the impression of spindly legs and massive fangs. She knew it was a hangover from the hallucinogenic drug she'd been given, but it did nothing to settle her unease.

Hudson arrived at a small jetty and walked briefly along before tailing off into the greenery behind it. He'd had to jump and land on a bank that was not easily accessible. The water lounged in past the jetty and then formed an almost horseshoe around the spit of land that Hudson was on. He would have needed to walk a longer way around to get to there, and she understood why he'd taken the jetty to do it quickly.

Hudson took out a pair of binoculars and started scanning the water. Kirsten looked off into the night and could see a white light coming towards them. It stopped some distance away, and clearly, Hudson was watching this arrival. The boat looked like a tiny fishing vessel, and it came alongside the jetty before berthing, two men jumping out and tying berthing lines. A third man got off with them. Hudson kept his binoculars trained while Kirsten, further away, was struggling to see their faces.

They walked along the jetty, chatting happily to each other before heading for the path. Hudson, at this point, had put down the binoculars and was rummaging in his pocket. He'd taken his eye off the departing fishermen. They were closer to Kirsten, and she was having to stay low, remaining in the dark while they passed by. Between watching Hudson and the sailors, she was almost caught out. For one minute they were on the path, and she could see Hudson, and then the men were gone.

Kirsten scanned into the greenery and caught a white shirt moving in the dark. It was the man who had tied up the far berthing line, and as she watched him, her eyes adjusted, and she could see the other two. They were taking the long way round to the spit of land that Hudson knelt on. Hudson had his eyes trained on the boat, unaware of their approach. The three fanned out, so they would come at him from slightly different angles.

What should she do? Intervene? But why? Why were they after Hudson? Why was he here for this trawler? The man was a film director, albeit an erotic one.

Kirsten sat tight. She drew her weapon out, briefly checking it, ready to pounce if she needed to. If they drew weapons, what should she do? Defend Hudson? If he drew one back, defend the men? She didn't know the allegiances or the intentions of anyone there, so she decided to remain hidden and be a spectator.

Slowly, the men crept forward, the one in the white shirt taking the lead. They were a good twenty metres away from Hudson, and for a moment, it looked as if he was going to turn around. The men froze, and Kirsten watched intently. They didn't seem to have any guns, but that would not matter, for they had the upper hand. He didn't know they were coming, and all they had to do was remain quiet, be stealthy in their approach, and soon they'd have him.

What they were going to do with him and where they would take him, she wasn't sure. *There were no cars at the end of the track, or were they going to be picked up, or would they take him back on board the boat? Why had the boat stopped off? Was this a meeting? Was Hudson here to pick something up?*

He'd gone into the Taverna the previous time she'd followed them. Kirsten was itching to get stuck into this case. She was itching to blow it apart, to understand why Lobo had died. *Patience*, she told herself. *Patience. Watch the players; see what's going on.*

The men were now less than five metres from Hudson, and he didn't seem to have spotted them. In fact, he picked up his binoculars and Kirsten saw the men ready to pounce. She counted. One, two, three, they moved.

It occurred to Kirsten afterwards that Hudson's timing was impeccable. He'd put up the binoculars. He'd waited until he knew they would move, and then he turned, producing a pistol from inside his pocket. Three times he fired, but each time, there was little sound. It was a silenced weapon, and Kirsten heard the crash of the men falling into the foliage.

She watched him turn, walk up to each of the men, and place another bullet into their head. He was making sure they were dead. *Was he an operative or just very street smart?*

He left the men and then jumped across from the little spit of land onto the jetty and climbed inside the boat. Kirsten looked around to see if she could get closer, but she couldn't. She listened, and she heard the clatter of rummaging. The man clearly believed he was now alone. It took ten minutes before Hudson emerged and he had a rucksack on his back.

Kirsten did not know what was in it. There was no time for her to think about grabbing him, but she wanted to know why he had taken it. *What had they been doing here? What was he doing? He wanted me to be in his films, but why? Does he know who I am? Is this a ruse to get me into a place of danger? He's already taken me up to his room. Maybe that was just a way of engaging me. Maybe that was the story being established for how we knew each other before he disposed of me.* It would be good spy tactics. She knew that.

She followed him along the path when he left, sat, and watched as a taxi pulled up and Hudson got in. Then she turned and raced back to the boat. Kirsten jumped over the side and then took the small steps beneath the main deck. The place was in turmoil. The noises Hudson had made indicated he had thoroughly searched the quarters below. Quickly, she went through upturned tables, food, and other items that had fallen. She pulled clothing out from small bunks, but she couldn't find anything that looked unusual. There were another couple of rucksacks. She wondered had Hudson borrowed one to stuff away what he wanted.

Kirsten returned up to the wheelhouse and looked at the vessel log. There were several names, and she recognised some of them from the list she'd found on Pacho Herrera's boat. But the man who had disembarked wasn't Pacho Herrera. She took some photographs of the vessel interior and jumped off the boat and ran to the dead men. Quickly, she photographed their faces.

It took her another ten minutes to get back to her car, and when she started it up and drove back to the hotel, she gave a sigh of relief. *What had gone on and why?* Hudson knew, and she needed to get inside Hudson's head. Either by wooing him or by the old-fashioned method, strapping him to a chair and knocking it out of him.

Kirsten had to wind the car window down, and as she drove, she let the air run through her hair. She was wet with sweat. Her hair was matted. She knew she'd go back to the hotel and have another shower. She couldn't keep clean in this country.

On arrival at the hotel, she parked the car where it had been left before, and then quickly hurried in through reception and out towards her own room. As she did so, she could look over at the bar. There was a lone barman. He was attending to one customer. Sitting at a table, holding a rucksack, was Charles Hudson.

He appeared to be going through some papers with a pencil or a pen. Part of her wondered should she go over, but maybe that would look too forward. After all, it was now two in the morning. Why would she be up? Why would she be there, and what would she be doing walking over to a lone man in the bar?

She would get him tomorrow. If he wanted her to be in a film for him, if he wanted an audition, then that's what she'd do. If he was alone, she'd find out what he knew.

Kirsten entered her own room, checked that no one had been in it, and then looked at the little microphone that Hudson had placed surreptitiously on her. It was still sitting beside the pillow on the table, and she played the snoring loop once again.

Who had chased down Lobo, and why? Was Hudson working against or for these people? What did this have to do with information leaving the country? Now, it seemed more like a basic smuggling racket, rows between rival gangs. The reason she was here was to discover where the passage of information was routing between Argentina and Uruguay. In truth, she felt more like the police. She felt like she was here to bust a couple of drug dealers, but whoever they were, they weren't messing about.

Tomorrow would be Hudson. Her options were limited. Her local guide, Lobo, was gone. She'd have to become more active and less the watcher in this scenario. Kirsten retreated to the shower, and when she came out, lay down on the bed, placing both guns underneath her pillow.

Blast the heat, she thought. *I'm just not built for this place.*

Chapter 10

Kirsten was not a woman to entice a man. She just was who she was; that's how she lived. Craig had been impressed by her when they'd met, but it wasn't because she deliberately flirted with him. In fact, she'd taken him for coffee and talked with him, relying more on her good nature and general charm rather than any sexual advance. But she wasn't blind to her talents in that department. She needed to understand if Charles Hudson knew who she was, or if he was genuinely just looking for her as a piece of meat for his films.

The following morning, at breakfast, she saw him taking up his place on the veranda, working at a laptop. Kirsten finished her breakfast and then wandered over to him, sitting down beside him in rather loose clothing. She had a pair of shorts on, her legs bare, but was also wearing a clingy top with nothing underneath. She thought he'd have to look. He'd have to get the idea that she could be one of those women in a film, that she was keen.

'Well, if it isn't Miss Hastings.'

'Mr Hudson, I thought maybe today I could come for one of your auditions.'

'Well,' he said, his eyes roaming up and down her body, 'that would be ideal. In fact, now will be appropriate,' he said. 'My wife has popped out this morning for some shopping. We could be a little less formal.'

She sat down beside him and stared at the breakfast before him. 'You haven't finished your croissants,' she said.

'Well, then, if you'll sit with me for a while. Can I get you anything? Maybe a glass of wine.'

'It's nine-thirty in the morning,' said Kirsten.

'Yes,' said Hudson, 'but often I think a woman auditioning for the first time needs a bit of courage, if you understand what I mean.'

His hand moved across and started rubbing Kirsten's thigh. She let him and gave the impression she was nervous. She let her hands shake ever so slightly, and when she next spoke, her voice was slightly raspy.

'It's not something I've done before—quite something to be a star like that.'

'Indeed, but you are quite the beauty. I think you'll more than wow my audiences.'

His hand went up and began rubbing into her side, just above her hip. A glass of wine was produced a couple of moments later. Hudson watched her as she drank it. He never finished his croissants before he stood up and removed her chair for her.

'Let's go up and see how things pan out,' he said. 'One thing I always say is that you've got to be keen. You can't be too shy. And always take direction.'

'How many of these movies have you made?' asked Kirsten, 'It's just you sound very knowledgeable.'

'That's because I am, my dear,' he said. 'I've worked on so many now that it's rare I find an actress who makes me delight so much in the films, but I'm thinking you could be her.'

His hand had moved up the inside of her top and onto her bare back. They went to the lift, and as they stood there, his hand descended, and fondled her bottom through the shorts she was wearing. Kirsten shivered. It took little acting.

If a man had done this to her in normal circumstances, it's the reaction she would have felt, except she would have clobbered him by now. Instead, she was having to stand there and pretend to be this pathetic waif. They reached his room and Kirsten walked into the lounge area she remembered from the previous day.

'No need to go straight to the bedroom today. Just go over behind that screen there and pop your clothes off.'

Kirsten walked around behind the screen. She removed her shorts and the top, leaving herself in only a pair of knickers. She had however stolen a gun down the front of herself, a tiny weapon, discreet, and she removed it now from where it was held by her underwear.

'It's always exciting to see a fresh face,' said Hudson. Kirsten heard him sit down. She walked out from behind the screen, an arm across her breasts, the gun behind her back. She walked slowly up towards Hudson, taking in deep breaths like she was struggling with what she was having to do. Then quickly she pulled the weapon from behind her and held it in front of him.

'Don't move,' said Kirsten. 'I might protect my decency now, but if you react, I will too.'

'But your gun is not silenced, people will come.'

'And I'll tell them about the pervert I had to fight off. Now, let's get down to business, Mr Hudson.'

'Indeed, Miss Hastings,' he said. 'Put the gun down and let's see you, let's see you dance, let's see you.'

'We're going to check out your rucksack, the one you took off the boat last night.'

There was barely a flicker on Hudson's face.

'I said I want the rucksack, the one you took off the boat, Mr Hudson. Or do I have to rough you up for it?'

'Some men would enjoy being roughed up by a woman in your state. Some men pay good money for that. Have you ever thought about it as a line of work?'

He was too cool, too calm. Something was up. Kirsten edged slightly closer to him. If he made a move, she needed to be there. Too far away and he might reach for something concealed.

'You would suit that work. Miss Hastings, I could just see it. We'll do you up in black, heels, and that, but I think . . .'

She saw the move. His hand went down the side of the seat and a gun was being brought up. Kirsten was alert to it though and had stepped to one side, grabbed the man's wrist, pulling it sharply, and the gun fell from his hand. She picked it up, now holding a gun in each hand and pointed them at him. 'Don't mistake me for someone who'll try to cover up rather than stand here and fire.'

She saw him swallow.

'What do you want me to say?' Hudson looked at her, 'You pull a gun on me, I pull one back. It happens sometimes in this business. Some mother is annoyed because they think I've abused their daughter, made them do this, that, or whatever, so I have to protect myself.'

'You do, but it was too good. It was too easily done, and you crawl off into the night dispatching people with a second shot, making sure that they're dead. You've been trained, Mr Hudson,' said Kirsten.

She was finding it rather disconcerting, standing in such a state of undress, but the man was deadly. She would not let any mild embarrassment overtake her caution.

'I don't know what you mean, really.'

Kirsten stepped forward, took the butt of the gun and slammed it across his face. The man reeled and then looked at her as if she was insane. She needed more ideas, something to taunt him with, something to push at. She turned and delivered the back of her hand across his face, causing him to yelp. His head turned, the side of his neck was exposed, and Kirsten hit him with a jab on a nerve that knocked the man out.

Once she was sure he was out cold, she looked around the room and tied him up. Fortunately, she found some rather gimmicky items from his movies. Maybe he tried them on the women who auditioned, but she took the laces for some boots, tied his arms and his legs down, and only then redressed.

She tore through the room, looking for whatever she could. There were papers from the films. There were his and his wife's clothes. She found a passport on the inside of his jacket. It said Charles Hudson, showing him travelling back and forth from Argentina to Uruguay. It showed many other countries where he'd been, some of them in Europe, but something about it just didn't feel right to Kirsten.

The people who made these films didn't crawl around in the night dispatching people, especially from a fishing boat. Why? She combed the room more carefully.

The floor sported a large carpet, but underneath were tiles. She walked across the room until she saw a tile that didn't have the surrounding grout it should have. She reached down. After some to and froing, she was able to pull up the tile. Underneath, in a large plastic packet, were several passports.

She opened them up and saw the man had several names and the passports were from several countries, but there was also another American one. Anton, Anton McManus.

She flicked through it, and once again, he'd been all over the world on it. Any of these could be false, but something about that passport spoke to her, gave her an idea. It looked genuine, but then they all looked genuine. *Was this his real one? Was this the one he used when he had to get out?*

There was a significant amount of cash down there as well, and three guns. Kirsten looked at them. The thing about each individual gun was it told little. They were ones you could buy, but the three of them together said something to Kirsten.

The Americans gave out guns like these, standard issue. She examined further the back pages of the passport of Anton McManus. Inside one piece of paper, barely noticeable, was a very thin piece of paper, held inside like the contents of an envelope. She pulled it out and had to study it close to the window. There were codes. Codes for passing messages, codes for making connections that were secure lines. It would've been hard to pick it up, hard to have seen it there, but if he ran, this passport was the one that was going to help even if he dumped the others.

It made sense, but she needed to know for sure. Kirsten placed a call on Hudson's phone through to a number in the UK. It rang several times and then it was picked up.

'Oliver's Dog Kennels.'

Kirsten almost smirked at the name.

'I left my Angus in several days ago. I just wanted to check how he's getting on.'

'And your name is?'

'Miss Hastings.'

'Ah, Miss Hastings of?'

'24, Mulberry Road, Swindon.'

'Ah, yes, of course, we've got you here. He's doing great. Is there anything we can do for you while he is away? Are there any words you want to tell him?'

Kirsten thought through how to phrase this. 'My uncle Sam, he talked about coming over to be with me. He might want to drop his dog off as well. I just want to make sure that he's correctly tagged. It says on his tag,' Kirsten gave out one code that was on the small piece of paper. 'I'm just wondering if that's correct or if you know if that would be a misprint.'

'We'll certainly look for you. Just hold the line a minute.'

Kirsten watched Hudson, wondering if he was going to wake up soon. She could always jab him awake if she needed to, but for now, he was very docile.

'Hello, Miss Hastings,' said a voice.

'Yes,' she said, but her heart was jumping. It was Justin Chivers on the other end of the line. The original operator had obviously realised not only who she was, but also that what she was asking was to do a cover check of an American.

'I believe we saw those codes recently. The dog tags certainly would indicate that the animal is coming from the right place. I would say it's probably had quite an excellent history, and in terms of the breed, it's a rather friendly one. One you probably should communicate well with if you want to get anywhere with it.'

'That's brilliant,' said Kirsten. 'Give my love to Angus. Remember, he likes walks at least three times a day.'

'Well, we always aim to please,' said Justin Chivers on the other end, and Kirsten put the phone down. So, Hudson was an American agent. Now she needed to know what the hell he was doing here.

Chapter 11

Kirsten sat on the small wooden chair, staring at Hudson. He'd stayed out cold for half an hour, and in that time, she'd stripped him down to his underwear. She hadn't been sure anybody wore those big white vests anymore, but now she knew Hudson did. The hotel room was warm, and she felt herself sweating, but she needed to concentrate. She stood up, walked over to Hudson, and hit him several times until he woke up.

'You bitch, you're not going to work in film if you keep doing this,' he said.

'I think we can drop that idea. You're not just a man into films, are you? Anton, or is it Charles? Hudson or McManus, or is it one of those other names? I particularly like the Serbian one. You must be able to put on a good accent.'

'I don't know what you're talking about, but when I get out of here, you'll never work again in this place.'

'Well, you probably realised by now that I don't really work in that sort of line,' Kirsten spat. 'I think you operate in my line of work. I found all the passports, and I found the sheaf within the passport.' She saw his face flicker momentarily. He was keeping up a good image, but she could tell.

I checked with our people. 'Why are you out here? What interest does America have on this coast?'

'Why am I tied up then? You know we have a special relationship.'

'Our Prime Minister and your President may have a special relationship. As for me, I had to stand here with next to nothing on looking at you to find out what was going on. Trust me, you don't have an excellent relationship with me at the moment.'

'Really? I thought we were getting along fine, especially the view.'

She stepped forward and smacked him across the face with the back of her hand. 'You don't get to talk like that to me. You're either useful or you're in the way,' said Kirsten. 'I don't care if you're American or not. What are you doing here?'

'I'm here pretending to be a filmmaker, well, of the seedy type,' he said. 'I mean, there are worse jobs.'

She ignored his rather smutty grin.

'The thing about producing these films is I can travel backwards and forwards between Uruguay and Argentina. There's a route for drug trafficking operating this way. We've tried to close them down, but we haven't been able to do it. Drugs are often attached to such things as this type of pornography. If you can get close in, then sometimes you get offered the gear, and then you're able to trace it.'

'So, you're here to do what? Just bust open that drug trade.'

'Basically. Not so much to bust it open, but understand it. See where it's leading to, then the higher-ups will determine whether we close it down or what we do with it. A lot of the fishermen here are involved in it. They're running drugs over from Argentina. They stop in or just moor off the edge of the

Argentinian coast. Stuff gets dropped to them. They bring it over and they ship it on through here. It was pretty much self-evident with the amount of money being splashed around. Some of the fishermen here, they're not too clever. You don't take money like that and just spend it. You make it last.'

'That's what you were doing the other night.'

Hudson's face suddenly sank.

'Oh, I watched you. I've been watching you quite a lot,' said Kirsten. 'You went up to a Taverna one night. I don't know what that was all about. Then the next night I watched you, you were popping onto a boat, but not before you dispatched three people.'

'Three people who were coming to kill me. Three people who had decided that I was not to be trusted.'

'How did you know them?' asked Kirsten.

'I was making a deal with them regarding the drugs. I knew that this was a location they used. They'd said to me about popping into there for an exchange, but I went that night because I'd got wind that they were coming. I wanted to see what they were dropping off. They obviously spotted me. I mustn't have done a great job of hiding. You obviously did a better one.'

'I saw the whole thing.'

'You would, of course, have helped me if I failed to defend myself.'

Kirsten laughed. 'Was there anything else coming across?' she asked.

'Like what?'

'I don't know. My government believes that information is being passed about very important people in our country. Have you had any evidence of that?'

'No,' he said. 'No, but the reason I took a rucksack away last night was because I found something on board. Yes, there were drugs. I took that for evidence and to make it look like somebody had broken into the drug ring and ran off with the goods. But the other thing I found was in a small box, a protective box. It's an explosive, I believe, and I've sent it off for analysis. I think the box was shielding it. It's never good when something like that is shielded. It always makes me edgy, so I thought we should check it out. I'm also very confused about why it's on a drug route. Drugs make money, but shifting explosives like that, arms, it's different. It's not the thing that these fishermen get involved in.'

'Arms running not through normal routes,' said Kirsten. 'That's more like . . .'

'Potential for terrorism,' he said.

Kirsten stepped forward and undid the man's bonds. Her weapon was tucked back inside her shorts. Once she'd freed him, he stood up, asking if he could dress.

'Of course,' she said. 'Do you enjoy it, by the way?'

'Do I enjoy what?'

'These girls you bring up in here.'

'I'm a man; of course, I enjoy the view, but what happens with them isn't good.'

'But you just willingly brought me into it.'

'What do you think they do? Somebody like you is a better option. You might make a film or whatever, but you'll soon head home. You have money behind you. It was more of a fun thing for you, not a means to making money. Not a means to start a career.'

'Is that really your wife with you?'

'What do you think? Alison's my fellow agent. Look, I'll need to talk to my superiors,' he said. 'See if I can share anything else with you.'

'Of course. I've got a few other things I might share with you,' said Kirsten.

'Let's have dinner tonight,' he said. 'We can pretend it's you still lining up for my film. Wear something, well—'

'Sexy?' said Kirsten.

'Yes. Like the girls that come to do these films; they're desperate.'

'I'll see you tonight, agent,' said Kirsten quietly. As she walked out the door, she shouted back to him, 'Thank you, Mr Hudson! I hope that's enough to be in a film.'

She heard him chortling from behind but hoped that anybody listening in from the corridor would believe she had just paid her dues to be in a film.

Kirsten washed again, finding the oppressive heat almost too much for her, and then picked out a dress for dinner. Hudson took her two miles away in his car and they sat in a remote taverna.

'We come here often. Man behind the bar, he's one of ours; so is everybody that works here. The guests on the far side there, they're not our people, but I always get a table on my own and I'm able to record whoever I'm talking with.'

'I hope you're not recording this,' said Kirsten. 'My country wouldn't want to admit to my being here.'

'Right. One of those sorts of missions, is it?'

'Very much,' she said.

'If you look here,' he said and placed several pieces of paper in front of her. The top one had details about contracts and about working in the adult film industry, but when she turned the page, she saw names and faces.

'These are drug runners. Many of them operating the fishing boats, some of them operating taxis. There's a whole patchwork of links between them. I've marked up most of them. There are probably a few others still out there. What's quite funny is I've got some of them to finance my films. They're into anything that can make money. These are not the people behind it. These are not the core, and I think my company wants to wait for those—stop the supply further back. We're not looking to disrupt what's going on right now. Please bear that in mind with whatever you do.'

'Apart from the explosive you saw the other night,' asked Kirsten, 'have you found anything else? Any other signs of something beyond drugs?'

'Well, some of the boats are rather low in the water and I've heard voices on them sometimes. They're also providing actresses for my film. Some of them are not from here. They don't speak much, and in the film, they say little. They're not into that type of film, but I think they're from other countries. I reckon they're being trafficked through, and they make a bit of money on the side.'

Kirsten felt uneasy about this. It must have come across her face, for Hudson reacted.

'Look, I'm not happy about it either. I've already said we should shut this down, but they want to keep the link going for a while. If they're not doing it with me, they'll push it onto somewhere else. At least I don't allow anyone to abuse them during the filming.'

'Abuse them?' queried Kirsten.

'Oh yes. How familiar are you with what happens in some of these films?'

'I'm not,' said Kirsten. 'I don't make it a habit to watch this stuff.'

'Well, there are different layers. When you go back to the States and there are companies that run pornographic films, but all the actors and actresses are looked after. They're all on health programmes and . . . well, it has some governance to it. The stuff we're doing out here, some of the other ones, it's tantamount to abuse. I don't allow that. I say it's because of who I am, and often, the women disappear with me, but I don't use them. It's a fine line. That's not an easy one to walk. When we get proof of the drugs, we'll bring all the rest down as well. I've told them I want that.'

'You think your bosses will do what you want?'

'Do yours?' he asked.

She thought of Godfrey. 'Heck no. There's no way the man would do it.'

'You confused me, though,' he said. 'I wondered what was going on. There were rumours of an arrival, so I checked you out at the airport. You then went off to the embassy. That's not unusual. The cover story was good for that. Then when you came out here, you also laid up for a few days. I thought if I could get you into the films, I might learn more about you, and lo-and-behold, turns out you were watching me at the same time. The two countries really need to work a lot closer together.'

'We're in the intelligence community,' said Kirsten. 'Trust doesn't go very far. I've also had a fatality amongst our people.'

'How do you mean?'

'We had one working in the system. Got killed coming back to tell us something. We believe there's a major plot on the go, but we don't know what it is and how it's working. I then lost a man called Lobo.'

87

'The fisherman?'

'That's correct. I was out with him checking one of the fishing boats, and when I came back, he was dead on the boat.'

'I knew he'd gone missing. There was talk of it in one taverna, but they haven't found him?'

'No. If you hole the boat and make sure he is tied to it, he won't come back up for a while. Pity. Nice guy.'

Hudson gave a nod, which was about as far as you ever got for sentiment from an operative. 'What's your ploy?' he asked.

'There's a club in Buenos Aires, El pájaro raro. Our contact who was killed had a wine list from it. It seemed a very bizarre thing to be holding. I'm going to go to that club. You've given me some faces and images to be aware of. We'll see if there're any connections. I thought at first I'd stand here and watch from this side, but I think I need to go into Argentina to really uncover what's going on. Either shake a few things up or get in with the right crowd.'

'Well, if I can help you, make sure you tell me. If everything's tied up with this, it might be better bringing the whole thing down together. Look better to the Uruguayans as well. I know your guys won't care about the Argentinians.'

'No, we won't. I need you to keep me informed regarding the explosive, namely what it is.'

'You're worried it could head towards your country.'

'Names, very important names, and the whereabouts of those names at certain times. Now you talk to me about an explosive. Yes,' said Kirsten. 'I'm worried.'

She spent the next hour talking about the area with Hudson, less shop and more about the people and the culture. It seemed Hudson had been there a while, developing what had been going on for over four years. When he dropped her off that night at the hotel, she invited him into her room. She walked beside her bed, picked up the little microphone, and handed it back to him.

'One thing I don't get,' he said, 'You were on the boat, but you were in here. I heard you. We had you monitored, and I heard you sleep.'

'I clocked the mic when you gave me it. It was very good, though, very subtle. The pervert at my bottom, dropping the mic in. Brilliant touch. Next time, make sure it's the right person snoring. They've got some cracking YouTube clips of people asleep. Some of them are running for hours.'

Hudson gave a wry grin. 'Just take care,' he said. 'These people, they don't mess about.'

'I think you'll find I don't either,' said Kirsten. 'When the report on me comes back.'

Hudson smiled again. 'Have you been over our way?'

'Next time,' she said. 'If you haven't got the detail up by then, I'll tell you next time.'

Chapter 12

Kirsten paid a middle-of-the-night visit to the embassy to update Susan Dandridge, the Ambassador, on what had been going on. It also allowed her to feed back to Godfrey where her tentative investigation was going. Kirsten could also pay respects regarding Lobo. Lobo had been an agent for the local area, but he died working with a specialist brought in from Central. It was only right that she make an apology. Not that anyone was blaming her, but all the same, it was good practice. She would need these people, and who could say to what degree?

'Your show of respect is much appreciated,' said Dandridge, 'but what's your play from here, if you can tell me?'

If you can tell me. That made Kirsten laugh. *More like Godfrey wants to know.*

'I'm going to chase the wine list. We have drug dealing taking place and our American friends are on it. Boats are crossing with possible human trafficking as well, but now this explosive has been found. The Americans are looking into it, and we should know more about it soon. Given your suspicions that information about where some of our more important people are seems to come out of Argentina, that an explosive is crossing too gives me cause for concern.'

'As it does me,' said the Ambassador. She stood up and walked over to the curtains of the room. They were closed, but she opened them, motioning Kirsten over. Kirsten walked over, staying away from the window, and stood beside the drawn curtain, peering only briefly out to where the Ambassador was looking.

'Montevideo. It's fairly safe here,' she said. 'Although Lobo would've disagreed. I'll inform the embassy in Argentina that you're coming, but to be honest, I'm not sure how much help they can give you. It's much more difficult for them to operate.'

'Then don't tell them,' said Kirsten.

Without looking at Kirsten, Susan Dandridge asked, 'Are you sure?'

'Yes.'

'Well then, in that case, I'll wish you good luck. Is there any more I can do for you from this side?'

'If I don't come back,' said Kirsten, 'pay a visit to Mr Hudson. He'll have information we need to know. Probably better done at a lower level. I'm not so sure how much the higher echelons will want to give out that information.'

'You're forgetting our special relationship,' said the Ambassador, and then she laughed. She drew the curtains again and turned to Kirsten, holding out her hand. 'Good luck. Remember, we're here if you need us.'

It was quite a touching comment considering that there was no need for the Ambassador to say it. Indeed, she could just go back to her job and let Kirsten operate, happy knowing that the embassy in Argentina would be unaware. If anything happened to Kirsten, she was just an ordinary traveller cut down in her prime. Returning to the hotel, Kirsten packed her bag. The next day, she went shopping, picking out a few outfits that were light and cool, and extra luggage from them. They would be more in keeping with a classier outlook in Buenos Aires.

She flew over from Montevideo but routed via Rio de Janeiro before arriving in Buenos Aires. It was a long haul, but the last thing she wanted to do was get clocked coming in from Uruguay. Things had happened. People were dead. If she could distance herself from that on her arrival, all the better.

Kirsten booked into one of the largest hotels in Buenos Aires. She didn't take the top suite or any ostentatious room. Instead, she took a simple one, purporting to be a tourist who liked to have good accommodation while they explored the city.

She spent the first day walking around, passing, on at least nine occasions, by the club she was seeking to infiltrate. Kirsten bought souvenirs. She stopped in coffee houses and enjoyed local delicacies. When someone asked her what she was doing, she spoke of her deceased husband.

There was a special ring on her finger, and she hoped the disguise was enough. If your husband was deceased, you could stay away from men's advances, citing it as a reason. If they suddenly thought you needed company because of it, you could play up on that as well. It was also a substantial reason to go exploring. Kirsten liked the deceased-husband disguise.

She passed by the club late at night and it was indeed a hotspot. Many of the well-to-do were ushered in while others stood in a queue, most to be disappointed by the end of the night. You had to have money to be in there, but Kirsten thought she should go in slightly differently. She never liked to play on her looks, but this was a time to do it.

Back at the hotel, she dressed in a skirt that barely made it past her knees. She could raise her thighs up to the parallel in it. She could kick in it, but it looked classy, and it showed a bit of leg, a comment she'd first heard when she was training to be a police officer. Back then, Kirsten showed a bit of leg at one party, with outstanding success. However, she realised the guy was a jerk before she had taken him to any place he wanted to go.

From that day, she'd been wary about using a skirt, retreating into her gym track bottoms, and her role as a mixed martial arts fighter, but tonight was business. She was impressed with the cleavage she managed with the top she wore, and she set it off with a fake gold necklace that hung down at the nape. She didn't wear her hair up but brushed it out, hoping she looked like a rich man's piece of rough, the kind that some went for.

When she got to the club, she looked at the line awaiting entry to the club and thought there was no way she was queuing to get in. The previous night where she joined the line would have been lucky to get within ten feet of the door by closing. So Kirsten wandered into the VIP queue.

As she stood there, she eyed the three men in front of her. They seemed to be quite happy-go-lucky, and she walked up behind one of them, putting her arm through his, holding the arm tight.

'Do you want someone to accompany you?' She watched the man stare at her and then heard a comment from his friend.

'Wow,' he said. They were Americans. 'Where's that accent from?'

'Scotland,' said Kirsten. It wasn't worth lying.

'Wow. I've got parents from Scotland.'

The man bored her with various locations around Scotland that Kirsten knew more than well enough. Yet his descriptions of them weren't that close. She endured them, smiling and ignoring the hand disappearing down her back and pulling her hip closer. When they got to the door, the bouncer explained that there were only three people on the list. The young American looked at him.

'Well, I think it includes our entertainment as well, doesn't it?'

The comment was rude, but it was clear to Kirsten what she would be for the evening. The American reached inside his jacket and quietly handed the bouncer a bundle of notes. He gave a nod, and Kirsten was inside with the men.

The place was packed. Kirsten insisted she needed to disappear to the little girl's room and told the man she'd be back and to order some drinks for her. Instead, she wandered over to the private area of the club.

The dance floor was rammed with people, but she sneaked through and arrived at the edge of a raised platform. Beyond it were a number of private booths.

Kirsten bided her time, eventually picking off a man who had come out of the area and who was making a return. As he did so, she spun, tumbling into him, taking him down to the floor. She ended up straddling him in a skirt, making sure he would definitely notice her.

'Oh, I'm sorry,' she said. 'I'm so sorry. Are you okay?' She'd noticed he'd been single, hanging out on the edge of a group, bored, with nothing to do, and suddenly there was this woman.

'No, entirely my fault,' he said. His English was good, but the accent wasn't from the UK.

'Well, I'm sorry. It's my fault. I'm sorry, Mr . . .'

'Juan, just call me Juan,' he said. 'Can I offer you a drink, please?'

'You don't have to do that,' said Kirsten. 'Really, it's not . . .'

'I have nothing to do tonight. You're going to help me no end. I'm a bit bored. Come. I'm just in here.'

Kirsten walked through the small entrance to the upper area. Two men in dinner jackets nodded at her as she walked past with Juan. She thought at first that he was going to sit with the group he was with before, but he took another smaller table close by. He clicked his fingers, and soon there was champagne sitting between the pair of them.

He sat and asked about her, and Kirsten told him the tale of her dead husband and how she was off to live life and explore it. She was looking for new challenges, looking for new people in her life. She could see the man's eyes. Wherever she went, there was that mole who was hoping to get lucky. It was a crude way to put it, but that's what it was.

More champagne arrived, but Kirsten was careful with what she drank, filling his glass when he wasn't looking, and then dropping a little pill into it. It took twenty minutes before the man had fallen asleep. Kirsten stood up and wandered around the VIP area.

She saw several men disappear towards the rear and stopped one man, asking what was beyond there. He said card games for the people with real money. Kirsten had brought little with her. In truth, she didn't get that much from the service. She'd have to go in with several grand. She looked around her and saw the unfamiliar faces in the private area.

Quickly, she picked out a couple of targets. People who would have money, people who would have it in their pockets. Couldn't go for the ones who were too well off because some of them wouldn't carry cash. They would know who they were. Credit would be extended. She would need physical cash.

It took half an hour to bump into three different men. Her hand would slip inside the jacket. While she was apologising, her hand was removing money behind their back. Then, as she reached up to kiss them on the cheek and apologise, the wallet went back in. Macleod would be disgusted at what she'd learned in spy school, but she had the cash, and she approached the door. All she had to do now was blag her way in.

The man on the door took the equivalent of three hundred pounds bribe to let her in. She pointed out to him she'd be good on the eye, something he didn't disagree to, but also that she had plenty of money to spend. She flashed him the roll of notes, and he checked and counted them before allowing her access. Inside were seven men, all dressed smartly. Tuxedos, the best-of-line suits, and they looked over when Kirsten arrived.

'You in the right place?' asked an American man.

'If you play cards and you have money, I'm in the right place,' she said. 'I've got an inheritance to burn. Have you space at the table?'

She knew that sort of bravado spurred on men like this, and she sat down, taking out her money and handing it over to one of the smartly dressed servers at the table. Chips were brought back, and she noticed that her pile was slightly smaller than everyone else's, as in about an eighth.

'Are you sure you don't want a little extra to play with?' said one man. 'After all, we can then play a little extra afterwards.'

'Afterwards, I'll tell you, if you can entertain me enough to earn your money back.'

The table went into laughter. The man she had slighted was angry. All the better, she thought. You never play cards angry, you never play upset, and you never play overjoyed. You play on the level. When she trained as a spy on her various stakeouts, cards had been the thing to do. She'd never played for money, well, certainly not her own, but Kirsten could read people and she could read their tells.

As Kirsten was dealt the first hand, she clocked a face at the far end of the table. He was on Hudson's list but wasn't a fisherman, though. He was slimmer. Didn't have that build, didn't have that muscle from hauling the catch, from fighting the waves, from a life of hard work. Instead, his fingers almost looked manicured. He had skin that spoke of applied cream to it to keep it smooth. No one else there footed any of the bills, but the man had money, and maybe this was where he spent it.

As Kirsten looked at her first cards, she realised the aim tonight was to get closer to the man. The card game lasted five hours. At one point, she had to lose deliberately to keep the other man in the game. He wasn't a skilled player, and it was tough manipulating everybody else so that he would still win; he would still be there. After an hour or two, the men had left, including the one who had looked to insult her at the start. As he departed, she asked if he'd be prepared to do her a service for his money back, but all she got was laughter from the table and a scowl from him. When the night had reached three in the morning, there were only three players left. Kirsten, down to not a lot, the man she sought, and another older American. She could have won that hand, but she folded to let her target man win it. It only took twenty minutes after that for her to throw in the rest of her cash.

'My name is Alvez,' he said, but she knew that already. 'You've had a rough night. Why don't I show you a bit of a better time?'

'Here,' she said. 'Why'd you think I was playing cards?'

'Sweet,' he said. 'I have a yacht. We can go to it.'

'You expecting me to buy back my losses?'

'No,' he said. 'I'm expecting you to embrace your new life of adventure.'

Kirsten laughed. She put his arm around hers, let him take her out the rear door of the club into a limousine. She laughed, giggled at his jokes, and happily leaned into him on the drive down to the yacht. It had been a heck of a night so far, and she'd struggled to keep her alcohol level at a point where she could still focus. So far, she'd been successful, but the proper work was about to begin.

Chapter 13

Kirsten was impressed by the yacht. It had at least four crew onboard and who knew how many below in their cabins. She was immediately attended to by a man in smart dress, offering her drinks beside the jacuzzi on the top deck. For a while, she drank with Alvez, listening to him talk about his recent visits to various locations in the world.

She asked about the yacht and where he took it but found out that it was mainly moored here and only occasionally would it sail off. It was more of a work office, for he told her he spent a lot of his days here with all the modern comms to communicate with the rest of the world. In fact, he said, it was the best view from an office he'd ever had.

Kirsten smiled and grinned while he ran his hand across the back of her neck. Slowly he dismissed the servants and Kirsten reckoned it was getting to that part of the night where he would soon want to take her to bed. She found the tablet inside the lining of her clothing, took it out, and dropped it in his drink while he wasn't looking.

It'll be twenty minutes, she reckoned. She spent the next ten subtly encouraging him to retreat to his bedroom and then the next five encouraging him in a less subtle way.

The bedroom was in the middle of the yacht, on the port side, so he could look out. The curtains were drawn in the cabin, the lights were down low, and as she stepped inside, she felt his arms envelope her. He kissed her on the nape, rubbing his hands across her shoulders.

Kirsten heard the door close behind her when he broke away, and then heard a lock turning. She walked forward, spun around, and grabbed her top, motioning to pull it over her head. But she saw Alvez' eyes swim, and he tumbled off to the left, collapsing on the bed.

Quickly, Kirsten stripped him, placed him in the bed, and left him snoring. She'd seen security cameras around the yacht nestled here and there, but there were none within the bedroom. She checked the designer cupboards, finding only his clothes. There was an extensive wardrobe filled with suits, smart shoes, and other items a businessman would require.

She would not be watched in here, but she wanted to check out where he worked. There was silence except for the gentle lapping of waves, for there was only a light wind tonight. The harbour walls would break any sea swell.

Kirsten noticed that the windows at the side of the bedroom could be opened. That gave her an idea. The corridor she had come along had a security camera on it. She believed the operations room for all the cameras was a room she'd seen towards the rear of the vessel. Alvez had taken her on a tour showing her the vessel, but there was one room she hadn't been allowed into. *Surely the operations ran from there, but would it be manned at night?*

Kirsten lost her shoes and clambered out of the window, cool air running across her body. She'd had some drinks, but she felt perfectly alert. There were other vessels berthed nearby, but she was confident that no one was about on the nearby jetties. In the city, nowhere ever truly goes quiet, but here, nobody was looking at the side of a yacht to see if anyone was crawling out.

Kirsten clambered along the side, holding on by her fingertips at times, until she reached the aft of the vessel which was an open deck. She had spotted a camera, but it was on her side, and so when she clambered right onto the deck, she was able to route underneath it, slipping towards the door. The operations room was just inside there.

Now came the genuine risk of what she was doing. Would there be someone there? She opened the door quickly, ready to race forward and strike, but she came upon an empty room. It was a tight cupboard, in a lot of ways, but before her was a recording machine, keyboard, and screens, and she could see every part of the vessel. The system wasn't that dissimilar to those she had practiced on when she was training for the service, and she assumed she could locate the files that were stored since her arrival.

She quickly deleted these and then began switching off the cameras. She'd switch them back on before she left. With any luck, they wouldn't have any reason to check them. It was one thing to have her face identified as being on board. However, she didn't want to give them reason to think she was anything more than a woman on holiday having a good time.

Kirsten exited the surveillance room and searched the upper deck, for surely that was where Alvez would work from. The servant's quarters were usually located down below, and she walked to the comprehensive study Alvez had showed earlier on her tour. He hadn't taken her inside and when she got to the door; it was locked.

Quickly, she made her way back to the surveillance room. Kirsten opened up several panels to see if there was a failsafe emergency opening for the lock and found it located down low. It masqueraded as a device for setting off the ship's siren. She tapped it, walked quickly back along the corridor, and was in the study inside of twenty seconds.

There was a large desk complete with a leather chair and Kirsten could visualise the man working away at whatever scheme he was on. There was a computer which she didn't want to touch. Instead, she started rifling through what paperwork was around. Unfortunately, Kirsten found nothing but standard business transactions or memos from business meetings.

Five minutes later, disgruntled, she left the office, and began searching the rest of the ship. The deck she was on contained rather mundane dens and private rooms for Alvez. None of these contained anything of note, simply somewhere for him to be entertained. Kirsten descended to the lower decks.

She passed through what must have been the staff quarters because she could hear snoring behind doors. However, there was a further deck below. When she reached it, she realised it was locked. This intrigued Kirsten. On the staff deck, there were basic locks, but nothing that required an electronic override to get through.

She glanced at her watch; it was now nearly four in the morning. She'd maybe have another half hour, an hour at most, before Alvez would wake up. When he did, she wanted to be there so he could identify that he'd been with her, even if he couldn't remember the night.

Kirsten strode quickly back up to the surveillance room. Once inside, she began checking panels and found a button that would release the lock on the lowest deck. After pressing it, she walked down the decks and into what seemed like a cargo bay. The lowest deck of the vessel had racking along one side, as well as a small area with a table, chairs, and a drinks cabinet beyond them.

Kirsten started checking the racking, finding large, heavy boxes, the type used by the military. She unclasped one box and found an array of machine guns inside. Kirsten opened more crates and found hand grenades and other weapons, and then, in one, she found money. There was such a myriad of notes that she decided not to count.

Alvez obviously dealt in arms to some degree. She walked to the desk, sat down, and started looking through the paperwork on top. A lot of it seemed to be code. She pulled out some drawers at the desk, found several notebooks, and scanned through them. She stopped at one.

There was a list of destinations, all as far as she could remember, on the east side of Argentina, and she thought, quite close to here. She committed them to memory, going through each one, taking the time to sit and let it sink in, aware that the clock was still ticking. Alvez would wake up, his drug-induced sleep would end, and Kirsten needed to be back.

She was struggling to understand how Alvez could be involved in her investigation. She was looking for some-one sending information across, but this man looked like a weapons smuggler. Who were the people he dealt with? Maybe he was into drugs as well, and that's why he was on Hudson's list. Was she just doing the work for the Americans that they decided not to do themselves? Hudson couldn't have got into this sort of boat, and to get one of his ladies to worm her way in here would be difficult.

Alvez was clearly someone at ease with being in Buenos Aires. *Did he have somebody looking after him? Was someone in the government making sure that no one was looking into his affairs?* There was plenty of security in one sense on the boat, but it was a boat. There was nothing to stop anyone jumping on board in the middle of the night and running amok with a gun. Clearly, he was at ease with where he was, or maybe he was just unknown. She didn't believe that.

Kirsten decided her time was up. She placed the books from the drawers back in. She checked that the lower deck was left as she'd found it, switched off the lights, and closed the hatch before making her way back up through the decks. As she reached the staff deck, a door opened at the end of the corridor.

Opening the door behind her, she stepped inside what she discovered to be a toilet cubicle. She listened intently and heard footsteps coming her way. She didn't need this. Time was of the essence, and she needed to get back. She needed to be with Alvez when he woke up, but she was now trapped in a toilet. The spy's life was just so full of glamour.

The footsteps weren't stopping. Kirsten put her arms on the wall in front of her, her feet at the back, and climbed up the small cubicle. She reached the roof, flattened herself out as best she could, keeping clear where the door would open. There was just a chance that if whoever ever came in, they would be so dog-tired, so sleepy that they'd simply look down, look at the toilet.

The door opened and a man in a hoodie wandered in. He had boxer shorts on. Kirsten watched as he lifted the toilet lid and did his ablutions. The hood was a godsend. It would keep his eyes focused forward, and most people wouldn't lift their head, especially inside at this time of day.

She watched as he turned, opened the door, and left, and she criticised him for not washing his hands. Once she'd heard him go through another door, Kirsten crawled back down and stood waiting in the toilet. Thirty seconds later, she'd heard no sound. Kirsten opened the door, closed it silently behind her, and raced as quickly as she could back up to the surveillance cabin.

Once inside, she flicked on all the surveillance cameras again, making sure all the locks were reset. Then Kirsten strode out under the camera on the rear deck that opened up to the side of the ship. It was still dark, thankfully.

The wind was picking up. She felt a chill through her top as she crawled along the side of the vessel before finding the window that she'd left, closed, but certainly not locked. As she clambered in, she saw Alvez stir. Carefully, she stepped over him, the window on the other side, and as she closed it, he muttered.

With one hand, she ran a finger around his ear and then down his neck. He murmured. Her other arm was freeing herself from the top, and she soon dumped it on the floor. Alvez was stirring now, about to turn over, and she dropped the skirt she was in, as well as her underwear. He moaned, gave his head a shake, and then looked up at her.

Kirsten stood fully naked before him, and she walked forward, wrapping herself around him.

'Did I wake you?' she asked. 'Sorry, I've got to go. I need to be somewhere this morning. Got a friend to meet. That was terrific. You really are quite something.'

She felt his arms pull her close, kissing her, and then she watched as he stared as she dressed herself. He pressed a button and the cabin door opened and one of his crew stood there, smartly dressed.

'Miss Hastings will be leaving. Take her wherever she needs to go,' said Alvez. 'Will you be about?'

'I'll be departing soon,' said Kirsten, 'but really, I think I'll spot this yacht wherever I go. Are you sailing anywhere soon?'

'Not that I can think of,' he said. 'Leave a number with Alejandro and we'll maybe get in touch.'

Kirsten smiled and then Alejandro escorted her off the yacht and down to where there were waiting taxis. The man took out some money, handed it to the taxi driver, explaining something to him. The driver turned around and asked where to. Kirsten gave her hotel and then waved to Alejandro, looking like a woman who'd had the night of her life. In truth, she was dog tired, exhausted from running around, exhausted from getting into the club and performing all night in front of these rich men. She needed a bath; she needed sleep, but she knew what she really needed to do. Kirsten had to get the names that she had memorised written on paper and then off to the service.

Chapter 14

Kirsten sat in front of the hotel desk with a pencil and a piece of paper. It took her fifteen minutes to regurgitate from her mind all the destinations that she had seen. When she'd written them all down, she took her phone and sent off a message to a secure address. Having done that, she burnt the paper she'd written the names down on, went into the bathroom and ran herself a bath. She lay in it for half an hour and then got worried she'd fall asleep. Five minutes later, after drying herself and placing two guns underneath her pillows, she fell asleep.

When Kirsten awoke, she checked her watch. She was lucky if she had four hours' sleep, and it felt like it, her limbs tired. She rolled over and grabbed her phone. There was a message there, 'Playa Reserva Ecológica, Buenos Aires,' and a time for a meeting that night at ten. That would mean five, teatime; you never sent the real time over. Depending on who you were working with, they could have a change in the time code. Kirsten's was a 'five-hour previous' currently.

She dressed, went downstairs, and ate in the hotel, then took herself shopping just in case anyone was watching. Kirsten made it back for four o'clock and then caught a taxi out to the ecological reserve that had been stated in the message. She dressed in some light slacks with a bag at her side and a T-shirt on top. She was hoping to look like a tourist. After all, the reserve was a good place to go.

The reserve was basically a large piece of land with plenty of trees and wildlife. It wasn't there to hold large animals; it was there to hold the small ones. A bastion beside the large concrete jungle of Buenos Aires. There were a couple of paths that led out round it, but for the most part, the centre of it was left to the wildlife.

She came to the entrance and stood looking around to see if she could find anyone she recognised, but they hadn't specified a particular part of the reserve. That being the case, she walked down one path. It was their job to find her, not the other way round. After all, she didn't know who was coming.

It went past five o'clock and Kirsten had found no one. She strolled along the long path out to the far end of the reserve. As she turned a corner, able to see Uruguay across the bay to the east of Buenos Aires, she saw someone coming, walking the path from the opposite direction. They were in a sharp suit, a Panama hat on top, but their gait gave them away.

Justin Chivers had a walk that he could switch on and off. Justin had almost a skip in the way he moved, and it was distinctive. Being the spy he was, he could drop it at the touch of a hat, but he could also switch it on when he needed to convey who he was to someone else.

Kirsten held back a smile. She hadn't been down in South America that long, but it was good to know that Justin was in the area. She'd worked with him in Inverness, and he was thorough. Indeed, he'd helped save them when they were out in Zante. Somewhat of a maverick, he was always watched with a little suspicion by the service. But his talents were also recognised.

'Lovely part of the world,' he said as she walked past him.

'You're the first living soul I've seen.'

'Not quite the same for me,' he said. 'You wouldn't happen to have a lighter, would you?'

Justin produced some cigarettes, and Kirsten froze for a moment. She didn't have one, but she said, 'Of course,' and reached inside her bag to pretend to proffer something to him. Justin, prepared as ever, had a lighter in his hand.

'Thank you,' he said, and lit up a cigarette. Justin didn't smoke, but they had to have some reason to stop.

'The destinations you sent over,' he said quietly, 'they're all close to players we've got an eye on, people the service are interested in.'

'But not so interested you thought you would share it with me?'

'You know how Godfrey works, compartmentalise it all. He sent you in with a clean bill of health, open eyes. You're not tainted by what's gone on before. The fact you seem to have come up with someone that links in is all good.'

'Of course. Anyway, I'm just here doing my job and getting paid,' she said.

'As am I,' said Justin. 'Good to see you, though.'

It was good to see Justin as well. Kirsten had missed working in a team. On your own was different, more difficult in some ways. She missed that light banter that she had working with others. With Craig not being himself, she had felt more alone than ever before.

'So, what's our move?' she asked.

'Well, looking at the names, you've got Moreau. He could be difficult to get to. Likes his music, but we haven't really got a way in. Cora, we won't get near. He's too protective, paranoia, almost, thinks the likes of you and me are around him all the time.'

'Imagine,' said Kirsten.

'However, there are a few others. Johnson had an American father, an Argentinian mother; he likes his fishing—possibilities there of me getting a way in. Then there's a guy called Marcelo Paz. He's a film buff.'

'Film?' said Kirsten. 'Does he like erotica?'

'Not sure. I'd need to have a look.'

'Does he like to invest in film?'

'Most definitely.'

'Well, Hudson, an American friend I met on the other side, he has offices here. He's been getting drug runners to subsidise his filmmaking before the Americans break them all down. Hudson has the cover. He also brought me in to star in one of his films.'

'If I was of a different persuasion,' said Justin, 'I could find that rather disconcerting, certainly a little off-putting when I'm trying to focus.'

Kirsten smiled. 'I didn't appear in any films.'

'Not yet,' he said. 'When Godfrey needs.'

'Shush,' she said. 'But I could think of a way in there.'

'Good idea. Contact Hudson then. See if I can work an opportunity, get some more detail.'

'I'll leave tomorrow morning,' she said, 'back to Montevideo. I'll talk to Hudson and make contact through the embassy.'

'All right,' said Justin, 'I'll just get on my way. There's a chap following me, a bit behind.'

Kirsten smiled, put her hand out for Justin to shake it. As he did so, she said quietly, 'Is he 6 foot tall?'

'No.'

'Well, then he's got company.'

She could see Justin looking around without letting people know that was what he was doing. Subtle turns of the head, all in the keeping of a man saying goodbye.

'I can handle him; you get out of here. Maybe go tonight instead.'

Kirsten nodded and began her walk back round the long road of the ecological reserve. As she walked away, however, she saw them, at least three people in the undergrowth. She continued to walk until she was out of sight of the hidden people. Then a man passed her coming the other way. She let him go and then stopped. *There was at least five*, she thought. *Justin's good, but not that good.*

Kirsten left the path, running through the brush and the scrub, avoiding where the ground was damp. Soon, she came close to where she had left Justin, and she could see the three figures in the undergrowth. She took her gun from her bag and checked the silencer on the front end. Slowly, she crawled in behind the concealed group of three and saw they were waiting at a bend. It was a point in the path where Justin would soon walk. He would be unaware of anybody being off the path. That's where they would jump him. He'd talked to me, and they would want to know what he was doing. Who they were was another matter.

Kirsten was bothered. She'd been made, or at least, Lobo had, in Uruguay. Now, Justin was made here. She had come in separately. Maybe it wasn't her. Possibly the contacts being leaked were not about her. Maybe whoever was leaking about the important persons in the UK had other information. Kirsten would have been on the outside, though. Very few people knew about her.

Kirsten stayed hunched down, watched as the men also awaited Justin's arrival. She raised her gun, ready to fire as she heard the crunch of feet along the path.

Justin strode along with a man less than a few metres behind him. She watched as another man appeared from the other side of the path, walking the opposite direction. He got close to Justin, then reached to grab him. Justin put a secreted knife up into the man's neck. Kirsten watched his hands fall away. Blood spurted out, but Justin had sidestepped and dropped the body behind him. The man who was following was splattered by blood. Justin spun on his heel and threw another knife straight into the neck of the trailing man.

As he was tumbling, those in the undergrowth stood ready to fire. They'd probably tag Justin. Hit him on the shoulder, somewhere on the legs, take him down so they could still use him, talk to him about what had happened, drag out whatever information they could.

Kirsten didn't hesitate. There was a look of surprise on Justin's face as the men stood up to fire. Then a greater one as they tumbled, one after the other, quickly. Kirsten stepped forward as they hit the ground, firing again into each one, the silencer keeping the noise down.

'Well, that's interesting,' said Justin. 'I clocked those two. Where did these ones come from?'

'Saw them when I left you. Obviously, the spot to take people out.'

'Indeed, there's more of a swamp area just over that way. I suggest we do a little manual exertion and carry out some impromptu funerals. Make sure their bodies aren't found for a while.'

Kirsten put her gun away and then went over to the first man she had dropped. She bent down, pulled him up and onto her shoulder. As she turned, she saw Justin carefully placing another man over his shoulder. He'd stripped the man's jacket off, allowing it to sit on his shoulder so that Justin wouldn't get covered in blood. It took them fifteen minutes to move the five bodies into the swamp and then find a large stick with which to push them down under the water. Kirsten went to leave, but Justin stopped her.

'What's going on?' he asked. 'Did they make you in Uruguay? I heard we lost Lobo.'

'I was on a boat, checking out another boat, Lobo waiting off for me. When I got back, Lobo was dead, but nobody came after me. The only person who has followed me at any point has been Hudson, and he wasn't that subtle about it. Then again, he is playing for our side, at least, he thinks he is.'

'The special relationship,' laughed Justin. 'But seriously, you've not been made?'

'I don't believe so. What happened to Lobo is what would have happened to you. I think this is coming out of the same source, whoever's sending stuff back to the UK.'

'Then I think we better sort this out,' said Justin, 'and fast. Can't be losing good people like myself.'

Kirsten nodded and then disappeared quickly, back out of the ecological reserve and to her hotel. She checked flights for that night, packed up, and was on a plane back to Brazil and then down to Montevideo. She finally got into a Montevideo hotel that night at three in the morning. Kirsten made sure that access to her room would be something that would wake her up. She placed two guns under her pillow and went off to sleep, or at least she tried. Lobo came back to her, and then

Justin Chivers. She could have lost them both. Whatever game was being played was a nasty one.

It occurred to her that these sorts of things didn't happen back home. Back on your own soil, it was easier. Out here on your own, it was much more difficult than even being out in Alaska. Her mind drifted, and the last thing she thought of was Hudson. She'd need to arrange a meeting for the following morning, but that could wait until she woke.

Chapter 15

Kirsten rose, hired a car, and drove down to the hotel she'd been staying at previously outside Montevideo. When she pulled up at the front entrance and stepped out of the car, she noticed Hudson watching from the hotel foyer. He didn't come to greet her, however. Instead, he turned and disappeared back inside the hotel. She found him sitting on the veranda of the bar. As she approached, he stood up, telling her to take a seat.

'Back for more auditions, is it?' he said. 'I thought you were giving my films a miss.'

'If another audition is what you need,' she said, 'by all means.'

He took her hand and kissed it. 'That's what I like to hear.'

Hudson stepped around the table, put his hand on her back, and steered her towards the elevator. She found it comical now. Now that she knew who he was, this pretence of the rather sly movie producer taking unsuspecting women up to his room was laughable. Once she went into the lift, the hand dropped.

'I hope you don't mind me doing this,' he said. 'Better to talk in the room. Some of what I have to tell you won't be for outside ears.'

'What I have to tell you will be similar,' she said.

They remained quiet until the elevator reached Hudson's floor. He led the way to his room. Kirsten was soon back in the large lounge area outside of the bedroom, where many of the prospective stars of the films showed their figures. This time, Hudson merely asked if she wanted something to drink and pointed to a seat.

'Coffee if you've got it,' said Kirsten. 'Running a little light on the energy today.'

'I take it your trip to Argentina was successful.'

Kirsten took Hudson through a very loose version of what happened; how she had dug up connections with gun running and sites Alvez may run them to. She explained that one of the potential men involved was on her country's list of being watched, and she didn't think it was a coincidence. 'However, Marcello Paz will be difficult to get to talk to, except that he's a film man, and maybe you can do the introductions.'

'Are you sure he'll back my sort of films?' he said, laughing. 'There are some decent people in this world who don't want to film naked women.'

Kirsten was feeling more at ease with the man's company. Yes, his cover was grotesque, but she could see that he wasn't like that. He certainly was an excellent actor.

'I think he will. He'll look to get involved. I need you to set up a meeting.'

'Where is he? Let me discover him,' said Hudson. 'I'll need to find some way of bumping into him or realising that his money will be useful to me.'

'Magdalena, do you know it?'

'Over from here and down a bit,' he said. 'Southeast of Buenos Aires, along the coast. Yes, I know it. I might have a contact in there as well. We can do this,' he said confidently as he poured coffee. 'Sit for a minute.' He brought the cup over. 'Sit and listen to this. The item we found on the boat apparently is an experimental explosive. It's very volatile, which is why it was shielded. If I had have opened it and checked it, there's a high likelihood I could have blown myself up. The thing about the explosion is, though, it would've been massive. You need very little of this stuff to make a serious explosion.'

'What is it?' asked Kirsten.

'It's a very new compound. I don't understand the ins and outs of it. They're still filling the details in. It's currently designated as XXYHD3, which frankly, sounds rubbish. In the office, we're calling it "Boom" because it makes a heck of a boom.'

'Where's it coming from, though?'

'The tech boys are saying North Korea, and the rest of the office is putting Russian backing behind that. We'll have a sweep for more of it to see if anything more is coming across the water.'

'You think it's something that could be used?'

'I was thinking of your information going back to the UK, all your important people. You get this stuff close enough to them, you can end them. Seems to me that's a doozy for what they want to do to your guys.'

Kirsten sipped her coffee. It certainly was something to be thought about and reported back to Godfrey.

'One thing about if we go over,' said Hudson, 'I need to know how far you're prepared to go with your cover.'

'What do you mean?' asked Kirsten.

'Well,' he said, 'I'm doing skin flicks. Generally, it's women with nothing on, and then there comes a man, and yes, it's not very palatable, but it's sex on a screen.'

Kirsten stopped for a moment. *How far would I go? How far would I be expected to go? What would Godfrey say? Was the information worth that?*

'Get me close,' she said. 'Just get me close. We'll find a way out of having to.'

'Whoa,' said Hudson, 'I'm asking because I have to keep my cover intact. My cover gets blown, we're going to end up not taking down these drugs chains, and that's where my country's at. I'm keen to help you. I'm happy for you to tag in and to find out what you need. We're all fighting the good fight here, even if we come from different countries, but I need to know that I won't get compromised.'

'You mean I have to compromise myself, so you don't get compromised?'

Hudson gave a laugh. 'Kind of like that,' he said. 'I know it's rubbish, but I need to know where you stand.'

'I guess I can manage it,' she said. She thought back to the previous night. It was in the early hours of the morning when she stood bare in front of Alvez, just to convince him they'd spent the night together. She'd got lucky with that one in some ways. She was happier using her fists. Happier to be seen as a strong woman. Acting like a starlet, a wannabe film girl was pushing her to her limit. She certainly didn't want to have to give up more of her soul than she already was.

'Good,' said Hudson. 'I didn't want to have to come in and ask when we were in the middle of a situation. Better to know now if you can't go through with it because if you didn't, they may react rather badly. It all becomes a firefight to get out. Getting too old for firefights.'

Kirsten continued to drink her coffee, and the two of them passed rather banal comments until Kirsten left and drove back to Montevideo. She dropped into the embassy, asking about some issue with her passport. Soon, she was guided into an administration room where the Ambassador joined her.

'Good to see you're back in one piece,' said Susan Dandridge. 'I was certainly worried. It's difficult operating over on that side.'

'I'm still struggling, though,' said Kirsten. 'Everything I seem to look into involves drugs, gun running. There's nothing coming back about information being passed. That's bothering me a lot. I'm worried we may be getting played into something.'

'The information's good about that,' said the Ambassador. 'I can't tell you much more than that, but it's good. Godfrey says he's tested it, and I agree with him.'

'I need to tell you about something else, though. The Americans have checked the explosive that Hudson found. It's an XXYHD3 compound, experimental, they believe, from North Korea but being backed by Russia. I'm sure our tech guys will find out the truth of that or not. They call it "Boom" in the office in America because it makes a massive explosion. It's the only thing that ties into the idea of people's movements being sought.'

'Are you still intending to go through with your movie maker idea?'

Kirsten could see that Justin had briefed just about everyone.

'Hudson's up for it, although, to be honest, it's not the most palatable.'

'I thought they trained you girls for that,' said Susan, 'all spies, male and female.'

'I'm not a honey pot. And I'm also independent. I used to cover Scotland, the north of.'

'I know your history,' said Dandridge. 'If you go into this

one, you're going to have to go in wholly within the cover. You're going to have to believe in it, and you're going to have to act like it. Can't blow this one just because you get a little nervous about your body. It's a bit more than just showing your body to some leery person. I mean, performing like that on a film.'

To Dandridge, Kirsten didn't show any concern, but just gave a brief smile. 'Hudson's good, though, for it. He's going to set it up, so I'll stay in Montevideo while he does. I don't think I should be over in Argentina until he comes and introduces me.'

'You're not worried about your earlier actions,' said Dandridge. 'I understand you went to a man's yacht. That's where you got information from. What if Marcello Paz finds out about that?'

'It's a risk we're going to have to take. We're not getting far,' said Kirsten. 'To be honest, I find it a lot more palatable than having to get my kit off to maintain a cover.'

'That's your duty,' said Dandridge.

Kirsten found her to be curt and cold today. When she'd first arrived, Dandridge was very welcoming. She wondered if losing Lobo had turned the woman against her.

'Just make sure we come through on this,' said Dandridge. 'Godfrey's concerned, very concerned.'

'Godfrey's always concerned,' said Kirsten. She left and drove back to her Montevideo hotel, where she sat down in the lobby for the afternoon. She tried calling home and the facility that was housing Craig. He was down; he was depressed still. They were struggling to get through to him. Nothing had changed.

Kirsten wished she could get home, see him, but that was

just a crazy hope. How would she do better than trained professionals? Maybe she would break in where they had failed.

She took a swimsuit and went down to the pool in the hotel, completing several lengths. When she stepped out and lay down on one of the loungers, she saw a man across watching her. He didn't have the look of someone who was from any of the services. Instead, he looked like a man enjoying a woman's figure.

Kirsten felt her skin crawl. She normally wasn't bothered by this, but the thought of the film coming up, what she might have to do, was playing on her mind. That was the trouble with the service. That was the trouble with what she was doing. When she went to Alaska, she drove it. She was the one who came out with the resolution, could say what she would do, how she would do it.

Yes, she told Godfrey that she could turn down any job, but she'd accepted this one. Now there was only one way to get done, to get through, and to get paid. She took a towel and placed it across her legs, and then another one across the top half of her body. Kirsten laid back and closed her eyes. Still, it wasn't an awful life for all that.

Chapter 16

It took two days for Hudson to arrange a meeting with Marcelo Paz according to conversations Kirsten had with him. Hudson made contact not just with Paz, but with several contacts purporting a new film and a new starlet to be in it. When Kirsten met Hudson two days later, he said that Paz had agreed to meet her, and that Hudson had buttered him up.

'You better act like somebody who needs this. Somebody desperate. From talking to him, he sounds like one of those guys, not the business type.'

'What do you mean, those guys?' asked Kirsten.

'In this business, you get guys who are strictly all about the money. They don't care about the girl, don't care about the film. They don't care what's happening in it. All they care is they're giving you money; you give money back. But there are others who see this as more of like playtime. Girls that go into these films, they see them as . . .'

'Loose?'

'Maybe more than that,' said Hudson.

'Easy?'

'Desperate,' said Hudson, 'Desperate to make it big. Desperate to get more money. Desperate to have a name. And having worked in these films and seen the industry, in certain parts, it's far from a star factory.' He looked at her because Kirsten was giving him a rather annoyed look.

'Don't shoot the messenger,' he said. 'Understand, I'm like you. I'm an agent working for my country. I didn't get into this to do skin flicks. Nor did I get into this to surround myself with women. I just got sent here. Truly, I half expected to be holed up most evenings looking at some rather dull house through a pair of binoculars. Spend my time making notes on the comings and goings of some Russian diplomat. It's funny what life throws up.'

Kirsten thought about her own life, and funny didn't seem to cover it right now. She had tried calling Craig again and the institution he was in, but he refused to take her calls and the doctors said he was getting worse, angrier if anything. He was refusing any sort of counselling, and she wondered about going back. But she couldn't, could she?

She knew she had to see this job through. She knew that any abandonment of it now would provoke serious repercussions from Godfrey and also a goodbye to any further work. Life was pigeonholing her, and this is what she had to do.

'So how does it work?' Kirsten asked Hudson. 'What do I do?'

'You come here tomorrow morning wearing something provocative. We fly over. We book into a hotel, and then tomorrow evening we meet them. I'll bring you something to wear.'

'As long as it's not . . .'

'No. I'll bring you something to wear,' said Hudson. 'This is a part you've got to play. I'm sorry, it's uncomfortable, but you either play it or you don't. I don't go half-measures on this one.

123

He's got to believe. If they think I'm bringing women who aren't genuine, you put me and you put my operation at risk, and everybody that works for me. I fully understand how you feel. I genuinely do, but this is what we're up against. Look, we're going to bring them down and you're going to find out what you need to find out. That's it.'

Kirsten gave a nod, and then on the way out, shook Hudson's hand. 'It's sometimes hard,' she said. 'You play your part well.'

'I do have standards,' he said, 'but you know what it's like when you're an agent. You have to do things you're not comfortable with.'

Kirsten thought about the men and women she had killed in her time as an agent. She never would've been comfortable with that. Not back in her police days. Yet now, she almost was. She was almost becoming comfortable. Almost okay with it. Not just seeing it as necessary.

Time in the service had shown her that life was cheap. She thought back to Alaska. She'd operated differently there, had been totally in control of her actions. Maybe that was a role for her in the future. Maybe this wasn't what she needed, to be a mercenary. Other people insisting what you did was almost as bad as being in the agency, except, of course, you could turn down the odd job. At least before it started.

The following morning, Kirsten turned up at Hudson's hotel wearing long flowing trousers and a crop top which showed off her figure. She wore her hair down and had put on more blusher and lipstick than she normally would. Kirsten didn't wear makeup lightly and rarely wore much at all. But she knew now she had to look the part, and because of this, she'd got her nails done, a false set, making them much longer than usual. She preferred stubbier nails, less likely to get caught with the many activities she partook in, but here she was, looking like a million dollars. She laughed inside at looking like the cat's dinner.

When they arrived at the airport, they didn't take a plane over. Instead, a helicopter flew them into Buenos Aires where a limousine took Hudson and her to one of the top floors of a hotel in downtown. The apartment was swish. At Hudson's request, they remained there alone; as part of their cover, he would interview her that day. Apparently, that meant he would be engaging in sexual activity with her. After checking if there were any cameras in the rooms, Hudson produced a recording on his phone, blasting it. Together, the two sat quietly planning the evening while the sounds of an excitable romp continued unabated.

Hudson stopped playing the recording after thirty minutes, explaining to Kirsten that if he put it on for too long, it was wholly unbelievable. Then dinner was ordered. Kirsten was peckish and tucked into her food before she was shown the outfit she would wear that night. It was backless and had a long slit in the dress's side, meaning her left leg was basically bare. Hudson handed over some underwear, of which Kirsten noted there were only bottoms. She disappeared into the bedroom, came out dressed, and Hudson cast an appreciative eye over her. But it wasn't the eye of a man wanting anything. It was the eye of a professional checking that she looked the part.

'Good,' he said. 'Just make sure you don't look uncomfortable in it. Remember, you're flaunting. You're there to say, "here are the goods". He's going to want to know the goods are there.'

'Darn creepy this, isn't it?' said Kirsten suddenly. 'I mean, really?'

'Men with money,' said Hudson, 'can do what they want.

These particular men, well, this is what they want. Some buy expensive yachts. Many like power. Some actually invest it wisely. Just be careful. Just because he might be a pervert with money doesn't mean he still isn't a dangerous one.'

'What do you mean?'

'I said he'd want to see you. When he sees you, he'll probably try to bed you.'

'Are you saying I should?' asked Kirsten.

'What I'm saying is don't blow my cover. If you become a frightened girl who runs from him, fine, but don't blow my cover.'

'So, don't take him out the back and kill him.'

'No. Absolutely not,' said Hudson.

That night Kirsten was taken by limousine with Hudson to the small village of Magdalena. It was dark when they pulled up at what looked a rather grand house, albeit South American to the core. The house was low level, but had an extensive path of brickwork that she walked along before she strode up steps to the door of the house. It was heavy and wooden, opened by a manservant who led Kirsten and Hudson inside.

Marcelo Paz walked in looking like a blowback from Casablanca. In a white tuxedo, he had a red rose on one side and was soon puffing on a cigar while he sat down. Hudson approached and Marcelo stood up, shook hands with him, and then offered a seat to Kirsten directly beside him. Before she'd even spoken, he was running the back of his hand down the outside of her arm.

Hudson spoke in Spanish and Kirsten tried to follow, believing that he was telling Paz that she was a holiday maker, a widow looking for a bit of excitement. Yes, she was maybe older than some girls that he got, but her stock looked good at this point.

Marcelo ran his hand down the side of her neck, then down her side, across the bare skin that she was showing, his hand running down her exposed leg. Kirsten stood up trying to look proud like a peacock. She put a hand on his lap, which he seemed to enjoy as he smiled back.

Hudson began talking about films and money as best as Kirsten could make out, but Marcelo wasn't listening to him. He was constantly looking at her, constantly going further and further with his hands.

'You are an exquisite lady,' he said. 'I think you'll be dining with me tonight.' Kirsten gave a smile, but she could see that Hudson was bothered by this.

'I think we should eat together. We can talk more about the movie. We can talk about . . .'

'You want your money? You will get your money if she is up to it. I need to make sure that she will look good in the film.'

'With all due respect,' said Hudson, 'that's what I do. I've got the eye for the camera.'

'But I have the eye for women,' said Marcelo, breaking into English. 'Don't worry, I'll bring her back unharmed. She doesn't mind, do you, dear?'

'Whatever it takes,' said Kirsten, 'sounds like fun to me. Don't you think so, Charles?'

'It's Mr Hudson,' he said. 'Let's get one thing straight. I'm the guy producing the film. I own you. You don't go freelancing.'

'Stop. Stop. Stop, Charles,' said Marcelo. 'All I'm asking for is a night with her, a night when she can show me how she will appear in the film, how good she'll be. I have other people looking to give you more finance, so I'll bring them along. We can talk to them as well.'

127

'Why don't I join you in case they've got questions?' said Hudson.

Marcelo reached inside his white jacket pocket and pulled out a large roll of notes. 'You take yourself back to your hotel, go to the casino, enjoy yourself with this. Keep what you win. I'll have her returned in the morning and then I'll sign the contract. She's okay with that, aren't you?'

Kirsten stood up and then sat on Marcelo's knee. She wrapped an arm around him, kissed him gently on the cheek, and then around the ear. She turned and looked back at Hudson. 'It won't be a problem, trust me.'

Hudson reached forward, took the money, and put it in his pocket. 'By morning,' he said to Marcelo, 'I want her back by morning. We've got things to do, plans to make. She needs fitted for outfits. She has lines to learn.'

'What lines?' said Marcelo, laughing. 'I think anyone can grunt.'

Kirsten laughed, running her hands around the back of the man's neck, but inside, she thought he was a weasel. He was so gross.

Hudson was led back outside, and Marcelo motioned Kirsten should stand, before taking her hand and leading her to a car outside.

'We'll go to eat,' he said. 'I have a lovely restaurant that I own.'

A car was brought around, an open-top Ferrari. Kirsten sat on one side while Marcelo sat on the other. Two other cars appeared, tailing them as they drove out down the long road south of Magdalena. The cars drove quickly.

'Where is this restaurant?' asked Kirsten. 'Is it seafood? What sort of restaurant is it?'

Marcelo put a hand over onto her bare thigh, tapping it gently. 'Don't worry. We'll maybe have some quiet drinks somewhere else first. It's here. Not far away.'

He turned down a road that headed towards the sea and Kirsten noticed that the cars behind her pulled away. Obviously, this was his hideout, his quiet place. This is where he would take the women and keep them to enjoy them for the night. The road swept down to the coast, and they rode along the clifftop, looking out to the inlet that divided Uruguay and Argentina.

The moon was up with barely a cloud in the sky, and Kirsten could see a small house up ahead. Marcelo reached over, pulling a strap off her shoulder, exposing half of her chest. 'We're going to see just how good you are in these films,' he said, grinning at her. Kirsten punched him hard.

The car spun, and she grabbed the wheel before hitting him again. She pulled up the handbrake as his foot slipped off the accelerator, causing the car to stop. Before he could react, she was up in her seat and had her arms around him, holding his neck tight.

'If you want to live, you'll talk,' she said.

'What?'

'I said if you want to live, you'll talk. I found destinations along this coast. One of them is where you live. Our people say that you greatly interest them. If you want to live, you'll talk to me. Because if you don't, I will use you. I will put it out that you have been talking to us. You know what that means? They'll torture you to find out what you've said.'

'What people?'

Kirsten thought about tightening her arm on his neck. She needed to work out what was going on.

129

'Information,' she said. 'Information being passed. People are running drugs over, people are running people over, Argentina to Uruguay. But more importantly, somebody's running information and somebody's running explosives.'

'I don't know what you're talking about,' he said. 'Sure, I run drugs. Of course, we run drugs, and we may have trafficked people. We may bring women across. This is it. Hudson does it too. Who are you?'

'XXYHD3,' said Kirsten. 'If you don't tell me what you know about it, then I will bring all of my people over here. We will rip up your empire. Everything you've got going, we will close down in a night. We will hit you with everything except I'll leave you alive. I'll leave you alive as the informant. Tell me what you know. Tell me the truth and I'll let you get away. I'll let you go somewhere. Either way, it's bad for you at the moment.'

She could feel him shake. He wasn't used to this. She'd obviously played the poor British woman well. The girl up for a good time. She had been no threat.

'I don't know about the explosive. I only know about its name. Information I've sent with people. I've sent information along with people running the drugs. Little bits, nobody knows all of it.'

'But who's giving that information? Where's it coming from?'

'Someone called Goldsmith is organising it. Goldsmith is all I know.'

'And where is he from?'

'I don't know. I met him in Buenos Aires, at the club.'

'Which club?' Asked Kirsten.

'El pájaro raro.'

Kirsten was astonished. She'd been there. That's why the wine list was important. That's why Franco Manfrin had brought it with him.

'And you've met this man?'

'Briefly. He said he was Goldsmith. He's sinister. It may not even be him I've seen. He has many people. Let go; leave me. I have to get away. I have to . . .'

'No,' said Kirsten, 'you don't have to get away,' and she jabbed him in the back of the neck, knocking him out as she hit a nerve. Kirsten sorted herself out, the dress having not been the easiest to fight in. Then she hauled Marcelo Paz into the rear seat. He wasn't strapped in, lying there completely loose.

She walked over and looked down at the sea below. The drop was over two hundred feet. It would be more than enough. She got into the front seat and began driving the car towards the edge. With the door open, she jumped out of the car at a low speed. She rolled on landing and steadied herself. Kirsten watched as the car disappeared off the cliff.

'That's for every girl you've brought out here,' she said, 'especially the ones that didn't want to come.'

Kirsten began the long walk back to Magdalena. She had her mobile phone on her, and she sent a quick text to Hudson telling him to contact the embassy because she needed picked up. They would find a terrible car accident by the cliffs soon enough.

She looked around her and then tore off across farmers' fields until she could find a suitable barn. It looked like it wasn't being used now. She settled down, glad that it wasn't cold weather. Kirsten wrapped herself up in spare bits of material lying around the place. It took twenty-four hours before she heard a sound.

Kirsten stood up by the door of the barn, awaiting whoever was coming in. Slowly, the door opened. Someone looked around, a gun before them. She recognised the weapon, standard issue within the service. She tapped the door with an old code that she'd used in Inverness.

Someone tapped back the correct response.

'Chivers,' she said. 'Good to see you.'

From around the corner, Justin Chivers appeared in a Panama hat, shirt, and slacks.

'Caused a bit of a stir. Hudson's not overly delighted.'

'I didn't think he would be, but I closed the loop. I take it they haven't found my body yet.'

'No, it could be out at sea. I would say Hudson's got about three months. After that, they'd expect it to wash back in. They might ask more questions.'

'They can ask away,' said Kirsten. 'How are you getting me out of here?'

'Got a change for you in the car. We'll take a fishing boat tonight, sail across.'

'No,' said Kirsten. 'I need to remain. Paz told me that the information flow is being organised by someone called Goldsmith. He met him at the club, El pájaro raro, but there were other contacts there. Goldsmith might not still be there, but I need to make a move.'

'Okay,' said Chivers, 'I can't promise luxury like Hudson provides, but I'll get you somewhere in Buenos Aires. You think it's wise going to the club? You've been before; thousands of people have seen you.'

'We need to shake this up,' said Kirsten. 'The only success we've had is going at it. I'm over here now. Let's keep going.'

Chapter 17

Kirsten stood in front of the mirror in the hotel room provided by Justin Chivers. She took a brush to her hair, this time deciding to tie it up as she dressed in a tight outfit, trying to look the part.

'I don't think you're going to get a good reception if you go back.'

'I'm not sure I will either, but best to try it this way first.'

'And then what?' Justin Chivers appeared in the mirror standing behind Kirsten. 'It's not really my forte, but you do look good. You dress up well when you want to, don't you?'

Kirsten gave him a smile. She'd been his boss for a long time, and she certainly didn't feel threatened by him because she simply wasn't his type. 'Well, aren't you the one with compliments today?' she said. 'Let's see what I can do to get in. I might need some cover outside, though.'

'I'll be about,' he said. 'Anything goes wrong, as long as you get outside, I'll be there. I'll keep tabs so you don't disappear off in some car either.'

Kirsten spent the time securing the weapons that she had on board. Most were small knives. She certainly would not walk in carrying a gun. That would be too risky, too provoking if there were any of Alvez's people there. They might question what had previously happened.

Taking a taxi, she got dropped off a few streets outside the El pájaro raro club. Kirsten walked confidently towards the entrance and saw again the long queue of people who were hoping to get in. The special people, however, were going straight up to the two bouncers, having their names checked off on a list and then making their way inside. Kirsten stood up to the two bouncers, took out a small wad of notes, and wafted them subtly in front of one of the bouncers.

'I think not,' the man said. 'I wouldn't join the queue either.'

'What's wrong?'

'Mr Alvez is not very happy about you. That's all he's told us? That's all he needs to tell us, so I'm afraid it's goodbye.'

'You can't be serious,' said Kirsten.

'I'm very serious,' said the bouncer, 'and I'm the one with good English. My friend is next door, he doesn't understand English though. He'll speak in his own language. We don't want that. We don't want things to get messy. I like a quiet life, so please move on.'

Kirsten took the hint and walked away, aware that she was being stared at from the long line of people, happy that someone hadn't just walked up in front of them. She walked round two corners looking for a taxi and then a car pulled up. Justin waved her inside. Soon she was back at the hotel.

'Going to do this the hard way,' she said.

'Have you got everything, though? Are you equipped to go in?'

Kirsten unzipped the holdall she'd brought with her from Uruguay, which Hudson had passed on to Chivers, and Justin looked it over. 'Well, there're a few weapons in there, aren't there?'

'I won't be hitting them with my high heels this time,' she laughed.

'Be careful though,' said Justin. 'You realise they'll know you're coming.'

'How'd you figure that?' asked Kirsten. 'Alvez just didn't want me in the club.'

'And yet you're going back to the club after spending a night with him, and for what? My guess is they will know of you. You didn't get everything wiped when you were on board. You were seen at some point.'

'I'll be careful,' she said. 'But what have I got? I can't really go back in with another line and try to find one of Paz's other cohorts. I can't use Hudson again. That went sour. I'm quite lucky that Hudson doesn't come after me.'

'From what I hear on the grapevine, and that's all it is, they're wanting local girls next time, no fly-by-night foreigners.'

'Oh, well, one thing is for sure, I need to get in there. We know Goldsmith operated through there. Maybe not him or herself, but however it occurs, there are connections being made in that club. That means there might be footage; there might be something in there.'

'I'm sure there is, but be careful. For instance, what time are you going to go in at? The club keeps running almost through the night.'

'Five a.m.' she said, 'as the place will be clear. Nobody keeps going at five a.m., but I'll scope it first. I'll pick my moment. I need you to drop me downtown though, just a few blocks away so I can get somewhere where I can watch the club. Know that I'm okay to go in.'

'There are a few other blocks around it. You should be able

to get a good view down if you can find an empty house to stay in.'

'Who says it needs to be empty?'

'You're a bit more brutal these days, aren't you?' said Chivers.

'Need to get the job done. But don't worry, I won't hurt whoever's house or flat I take over. I just need to tie them up for a bit.'

'Not that subtle, though.'

'No, but it puts fear into people. Be better if they don't know I am there.'

'Anyway, the taxi is waiting whenever you're ready,' said Justin.

It was a few hours later when Kirsten got Justin to drop her three blocks from the club. She was dropped off a little distance away and was going to linger in the shadows. She had a hoodie top, but emerged from the car with her face uncovered, although she sat with shoulders hunched forward. Once she got to the block they'd identified as overlooking the club, she buzzed one of the apartments. The place seemed posh, and she picked out a French name.

When the owner responded, Kirsten heard Spanish. She ignored it and said hello in French, advising that she had a package for them. When they said they weren't expecting a package, Kirsten insisted she had one. Would it be okay if she popped up to sort out the issue?

The door opened, and she climbed several steps before whipping up her hood and pulling her mask up from the inside of the hoodie. As Kirsten approached the door of the flat she'd decided to use, the owner was already out on the landing. As she got to the top of the steps, the owner clocked her covered face and no package.

The owner turned to run, but Kirsten was already jumping several steps and running towards him. As he went to slam the door closed, she jammed her foot between the door and the frame. She then hit it hard with her shoulder, opening it and knocking the man into the room. She was on top of him in no time and hit him with a hard punch to the face. He sprawled on the floor.

She quickly searched the rest of the flat, but there was no one else at home, and then took up station beside the window watching the rear of the club. She put the man in his bedroom, tied up, a gag in his mouth. He protested, but she ignored him, confident that no one could hear him.

In truth, she felt sorry for him, but she was on foreign soil and she needed to get things done quickly. Back in Scotland, she could have taken her time. She could have set up safe houses. She could have contacted people and asked to use their facilities, pretending to be the police.

It was close to five a.m. when she thought everyone had left the club. She could see refuse lorries on the streets. It wouldn't be long before the sun came up.

Kirsten left the apartment, walked a block round up to the rear of El pájaro raro. She saw the security camera aimed at the back door, approached from behind it and ripped it out. It was a coarse method and if anyone was inside watching, they'd know she was coming, but it was a risk she was prepared to take.

Kirsten was confident she could handle whatever came at her, and so she opened the rear door and swiftly closed it behind her. Glad she couldn't hear an alarm, she checked it to see if there was a silent alarm on the door. She couldn't find one and cruised her way through the back passages of the club.

Kirsten located an office, but the door was open and most of the filing cabinets inside were easy to access. She knew this search would be fruitless. Instead, she checked the floor and the walls, looking for anything that would indicate a secret hiding hole. Kirsten continued until she'd found a locked door into an office. Taking out her lock-picks, she soon had it open, but inside there was a myriad of paperwork and computers. She ignored them. Searching around the walls and the floor, she looked behind a painting, because they were always behind paintings, weren't they? But there was nothing there.

Then she saw it; the extremely thin line in the wall where the paint wasn't quite set. It had been open before, whatever this was. Although the two sides came closely together, the paint wasn't smooth. The line was there on near inspection.

Kirsten dug in a small knife and pulled back the front face of the secret compartment and was presented with a safe. It wasn't a complex one, thankfully, but Kirsten had little time. She took some hard explosive, placed it on the front of the safe and then blew it. The door opened and inside she found nothing. Quickly, she turned to see the man at the door holding a gun. There was no time. He fired. Kirsten stumbled when something hit her chest. And then she fell over.

Kirsten awoke strapped to a chair with her hands tied behind her back. She wasn't sure where she was, but one thing became clear to her quickly. This guy wasn't that used to agents. Most people you can tie up similar to the way she tied up the man in the flat. A couple of good decent knots and a gag around the mouth. They would never get out. Kirsten was different, though.

They'd taken away her guns and the large knives she'd been sporting. Her backpack was missing. She wasn't bothered because all it had in it was equipment. There was no ID, nothing that would say who she was. Now that she didn't work for the British government, she didn't use their standard equipment either.

Kirsten looked around the room. There were four men. Two of them looked like heavies, a bit of muscle. One looked like he was organising and the other one looked like he ran the outfit. She could tell because when she came to, they were all looking towards him.

'Miss Hastings, I hear,' said the man. 'So good of you to visit my club again. I am Toro Devia and they call me "The Bull." I don't like people breaking into my club. People going through my stuff, they… how do you put it… piss me off? However, you fell for the safe. It's always good to have one that's not that difficult to find, but still believable. It means that people like you can come to my lap.'

He marched forward and gave Kirsten a smack across the face with the back of his hand. It was nothing compared to what she'd suffered before. She grinned back.

'That the best you got?' she asked.

He gave her another smack across the face. Behind her back, she produced from inside her sleeve a small thin rod with a razor edge. She was slowly working on her bonds. Often, captors would put a plastic tie around your wrists, which was much more difficult to cut. But they had used a rope and the sharp item she extracted from her sleeve was more than adequate. The key was to keep the focus on her, the focus on her face, keep an argument going, distract them at all times from what she was really doing.

She spat at the man.

'Not very ladylike. I'm wondering just what you've been up

to. My friend Mr Alvez says you were running around on his boat. It's not very kind, especially after he showed you a night. That's how they say it in your country, isn't it? Take you out for a night of passion, something like that. He can't quite remember how good you were. Maybe I'll find out later.'

Not likely, thought Kirsten. She scanned the four men in front of her. Toro Devia was a short man used to being in charge, but not a physical threat. The two heavies seemed to be dull, slow-witted, but they were strong. She'd need to hit them quickly. The other man may be able to handle himself. He was the guard, the backup, his eyes were everywhere.

'People like you need to be taught a lesson, a lesson on what to do when you come to a foreign country. I don't like spies, whoever they're working for. I don't know who you're working for and, let's face it, I'm not sure who you are yet, Miss Hastings. But you'll stay here until we identify that. We'll work out what sort of threat you are. If you turn out to be a proper threat, you won't leave here. If you're simply a rather poor thief or someone I don't want to worry that much about, we'll do something to you as a reminder to others not to mess me about. And we'll put you back out in the streets so that they know it. You might walk or you might get wheeled out.'

Kirsten thought she'd have to maintain the attention on her, but Toro was doing it. He seemed keen to intimidate her and she let her face go into a worried look, shying away from him, turning her eyes down, looking like she was capitulating.

'Right, let's get to this,' said Toro. 'I want you to tell me everything, starting now.'

Kirsten felt the bonds behind her go, but she let her hands stay behind. There'd be a time and a place.

'Who are you?' said Toro. 'Tell me!'

Kirsten didn't move. Toro hit her with the back of his hand again once more. She didn't say a word.

'Fernando,' he said, 'show our Miss Hastings how to have some manners.'

The large man stepped forward, and Kirsten took her chance. As the large man approached, she reached up from the stool. Placing one hand around the back of his neck, she drove the sharp knife up into his neck, puncturing him. One, two, three, four, five times, all done in a flash. She then pushed him backwards, and he fell in towards Toro, blood pouring from his neck.

Kirsten reached down, sliced the bond that held her leg, and then reached over for the other one. As she cut it, the other heavy was making his way towards her and reached down for her. She let the blade go from her hand, firing it up into the man's throat. He reared backwards, holding onto his skin, trying to stop the puncture from leaking out air and blood.

The other man, the one she was worried about most, simply stepped forward, more wary of her. She turned and took a kick at him, which he blocked satisfactorily, and then she threw a couple of punches. Again, he blocked them, but he took no advantage. *Maybe he isn't that good*, she thought.

The larger of the heavies was still writhing on the ground. Toro Devia got out from under him. Kirsten was worried he'd start looking for a gun. It was often a safety precaution in case someone like her got loose, but then she saw Toro reach inside his jacket.

Kirsten stepped forward, ignored the punch thrown by the third man, ducked inside, grabbed him, and flung him with all her might. She watched as he cascaded into Toro. She then raced over, driving her foot hard down onto the man's head, and stunned him as he lay on the ground. Reaching down, she snapped his neck.

She then reached inside Devia's jacket, taking out his weapon, and held it to his head. She kept the gun pointed at him as she walked over to the two. One was already dying, choking on his blood. The other was trying to get up, but his hands were around his neck, the puncture still there. Kirsten put him out of his misery.

Turning back to Toro Devia, she picked him up by the collar and slammed him into the chair. She placed a gun to his head.

'Five seconds. Who's Goldsmith? What's he doing here? How does he operate? One, two.'

Toro looked up. 'You work very well, but you're too subtle for the Americans.'

He turned and passively stared at the wall. She needed him. She needed the information, so would she shoot him right away?

'I think the Americans want to talk to you. I believe there's drug running going on, human trafficking too. A nice spell away in one of their prisons. One of those off-land prisons? The ones they don't talk about. The ones were they . . .'

She could see the man beginning to shake.

'I don't work directly with Goldsmith. He operates in the club. I know little about him.'

'You better find something or you're joining the Americans,' she said.

The man was shaking now, and she could see him beginning to think through what he knew, desperate to give her something.

'One, two, three, four, five.'

'He's . . . he had a drop-off. I don't know what was in it. I don't know what was going on with it. The fishing vessel, I had to get a message to the *Garabine*. It's a fishing vessel. I think they carried the last shipment.'

'Good,' said Kirsten, 'Anything else?'

'No, I told you he works out of here sometimes.'

'Who is he? What's he look like?'

'He doesn't tell me. He's in the club. I don't know who he is. He just comes like a regular customer. I don't entertain him while he's here. I just make sure that the other contacts are here.'

And he may not even do the meet himself, she thought. *Maybe he sends in a ringer as well to check them out.*

She gave Toro a slap across the face, similar to what he'd given her.

'Unfortunately,' said Kirsten, 'if I let you go, you can ring ahead. I'm going to do you a favour and not leave you with the Americans. But I'm on my own, so I can't take a prisoner.'

She walked away to the edge of the room, then turned back and shot the man twice. She wasn't happy about it, but she couldn't have anyone alerting those she was about to intercept. *Garabine*, she thought. *A vessel called Garabine.* It wasn't much of a trail, but it would have to do.

Chapter 18

Kirsten cleared the building after searching it and finding most of her gear. When outside, she placed a call on her phone and called Chivers, who was able to pick her up. Being sedated had confused her, but she hadn't left the club. She'd barely been in there three hours.

No doubt the cleaners would come in shortly. Or maybe they'd been warned off because of what was going on. Either way, the place was deserted as she departed. But her face was known now. She'd been made. Even though they didn't know exactly who she was, they knew she was not good news.

'I think we need to get you out of here,' said Chivers, 'in case people turn up the heat.'

'I don't want to be here anyway,' she said. 'There's nowhere left to look. The vessel *Garabine* is our route in. I think I need to talk to my friend Hudson.'

'You think you're his friend after what happened with Marcello?'

'I think I will be when I tell him about this.'

Late that afternoon, Kirsten flew out of Buenos Aires, this time north to Paraguay, before routing back to Uruguay. Arriving in Montevideo, she found someone waiting for her at the arrivals gate. He was wearing a black hat, dressed as a chauffeur. He had the name Hastings written on his little card. She went to walk past, but the man stepped across.

'Miss Hastings, Mr Hudson would like a word.'

'And if I don't join him?'

'Mr Hudson says he's looking for an explanation, in the spirit of a special relationship that's enjoyed between your country and ours.'

Kirsten would have an explanation, and she also wanted to talk to him. She also saw someone from the embassy watching closely and turned to the chauffeur.

'If you'll come with me a moment. The man over at the back of that desk there—he's in the white shirt with the pale chinos—I need to talk briefly to him.'

The chauffeur looked quite anxious.

'Oh, don't worry, he's from my country. I'm quite happy to talk to Mr Hudson. In fact, I need to talk to Mr Hudson, but I need to let my country know that I haven't just been kidnapped.'

The man gave a nod before picking up Kirsten's baggage and following her. She walked up to the man in chinos and said, 'Give my best to the Ambassador. But I need to speak to our American friends first. I'll update her as soon as I have something.'

'The Ambassador was quite insistent that you should report in.'

'I'm sure she was, but things are moving fast. I will get to her as soon as I've spoken to our American friends.'

'Don't forget who you work for, who's paying the bill.'

Kirsten stopped. *That was bad*, she thought. *The man's meant to be a lackey. He's meant to just pass on a message, and yet he threw in a threat. He's either a badly educated agent or he's a much higher pay grade and let something slip.*

'Tell Godfrey I need to see the Americans. And tell him next time to send somebody with a bit more class.' She watched the man's lip wobble. Then he gave a nod and walked away.

'Right, James,' she said to the chauffeur, 'take me to my film producer.'

'It's Jim, ma'am,' said the chauffeur.

'Jim, James, whatever,' said Kirsten. He didn't get it.

One thing about Hudson was he enjoyed the hotel Kirsten had taken up in originally. The man was still there. She wondered did they have some sort of deal with the owners. Or were the owners the Americans? Either way, she was taken by a limousine to the front door of the hotel where she was escorted out to the veranda, which was empty save for one man. Hudson was sitting in a white jacket, pale shirt, and was staring at her, but not with the friendliest eyes.

Kirsten walked forward, dressed in a light pair of slacks and a blouse, and gave a smile as she reached the table. She put out her hand and Hudson stood slowly.

'You didn't have to bloody kill him.'

'I did,' said Kirsten, 'but I come with glad tidings.'

He looked at her quizzically. 'Apparently, Toro Devia, who runs El pájaro raro, is now dead.'

'Indeed, he is. He gave up the name of a boat. A boat which did the last ferry for Goldsmith. A boat called the *Garabine*.'

'*Garabine*. Just *Garabine*,' said Hudson. 'Not the . . .'

'Do you know it?' asked Kirsten.

'Oh, yeah. I know it. It's one vessel we've suspected.'

'Well, we know it is for sure now. I think it wise if we have a chat with the captain.'

'Sit down,' said Hudson.

Kirsten placed her bottom on the seat, and Hudson waved over at the bar staff. He sat in silence until two drinks arrived. They were tall tumblers, Kirsten unsure exactly what she was about to drink. Yesterday, she had been tied to a chair and had to take out four people to make sure she could make this meeting, so there was cause for celebration.

'We can go after the *Garabine*,' said Hudson. 'Obviously you want Goldsmith. How serious is this?'

'You have the explosive that they brought over. It was trafficked across. We've got to get a line in,' said Kirsten. 'I'm bothered that something big is going to happen in the UK, and we need a line in.'

'You could end up blowing our drugs line.'

'I could, but I know the *Garabine*. I'm here for your help because you've been tailing these people, but also out of courtesy. You help me, I'm going to help you before I blow the whole thing wide open, and they all run. When we get him, the captain of the *Garabine*, I'm quite happy for you to interrogate. In fact, I'll let you do it with one of our people. I'm not the best at interrogation.'

'You seemed to have done all right with Toro Devia, although you seemed to have finished him at the same time.'

'He could have called ahead.'

Hudson sat back, turned, and looked across the green garden beyond the veranda. 'It's been fun out here,' he said to Kirsten. 'I do like this hotel, like where I'm located. I enjoy Uruguay. If this all goes down, I'll be pulled out and lost somewhere else.'

'Life of an agent,' said Kirsten. 'We can go hook, line, and sinker with this. You can extract all the way back along the line, find out who's running the drugs through. Goldsmith must be tied in with that as well. My thinking is that he may have established these lines to look like a drug run, when in fact it's more about information. It's more about terrorism.'

'A cover!' said Hudson. 'It's a damn cover. Running drugs was a damn cover for information, for more serious things being sent out. Unbelievable.'

'I think he actually knows you're watching. He may even know your cover as a film producer. I think he was prepared to sacrifice it. Sacrifice it all to make me think that it's just a drug operation. Protect his source. Protect whoever's passing the information out of Argentina.'

'We do it then,' said Hudson. 'We do it. I'll flog the guy, though. I'll flog the guy to get this information. Nearly three years I've been down here.'

'Three years of having to get women to parade in front of you as if they're in auditions,' said Kirsten. 'Can't have been the worst job you've done.'

Hudson laughed. 'Well, maybe there's been fringe benefits, but it's not a pleasant world. All that stuff, you know. In fairness, I'd be happier on standard assignments.'

'When do we go looking?'

'I'll give you a room in here,' said Hudson, 'but don't tell anyone you are here. Then you'll need to talk to your people, I guess. We go out tonight, soon as it's dark. I'll get a decent boat laid on for us.'

Kirsten smiled. 'Pleasure doing business with you,' she said, standing up. Hudson stood up with her and shook her hand. 'You can sit and chew the fat here with me for a while. It's not a problem.'

'Haven't you got things to get organised?'

'Yes, but, well, an hour of your company might be worth it.'

He gave a smile, and Kirsten felt a little uneasy. The man had said he hadn't really enjoyed the job, his cover, and the number of women around him all searching for a job at his whim and call. Yet he clearly appreciated women. Maybe not in the best sense.

Kirsten was taken by limousine back to the embassy, where she had a quick meeting with Susan Dandridge. Then she was chauffeured back to the hotel, found a room, and got changed for the night. She sported a leather jacket over a light T-shirt and some trousers beneath. She wore trainers and had armed herself. When she arrived downstairs to meet Hudson, he gave a smile.

'That's you, is it?' he said.

She looked at him. 'What do you mean?'

'You don't do fancy; you don't look good in fancy, uneasy half the time, but that, that's you, isn't it?'

Kirsten understood why he got the job. He understood his women. They walked down to the water, to a small jetty with a speedboat. Hudson had glasses sitting in the back of it, along with bottles of champagne, making it look like he was taking Kirsten out for the night. They toured up and down, remaining on the Uruguayan side of the river until Hudson thought he spotted the vessel they were hunting.

'That's the *Garabine*. How do you want to play it?'

'Smash and grab,' said Kirsten. 'We go get them.'

'They are close to the land, though,' he said.

The boat up ahead of them suddenly began heading in towards land.

'They've seen us and they're on the run,' she said. 'I think somebody wants to get out of here.'

Hudson turned the boat and put the power on. Slowly they

edged closer to the boat ahead, but it was near to some berths. Soon the crew had tied up and jumped off, sprinting along the jetties. Hudson pulled up behind them and Kirsten saw them disappearing off into the dark.

'What's out here?' Kirsten asked.

'There's a town just beyond, plenty of bars, but you need to be careful. This will be home turf. I don't think they're far away from where they live.'

'Tough,' she said, jumping off the boat onto the jetty and began running, panting hard. As she ran down dusty paths leading out towards the main road, she saw three men disappearing off together. One cut away, but not before he'd handed money to the other two.

That's the captain, she thought. *They didn't want to disappear without some hush money.*

She ran as hard as she could, turning a corner, and she thought she saw something in the trees. Kirsten slowed for a moment, staring, hand reaching inside for a gun. Then she was away after him again. The captain of the *Garabine* was up ahead and turning into a tavern. Kirsten continued, pumping her legs as hard as she could, and reached the tavern.

Reasonably out of breath, she stopped just short of the front door and pushed it open, stepping slowly inside. There was laughter and plenty of drinking. She saw the captain at the far end sitting down at a table. As he did so, he turned around to her and a smile went across his lips.

They knew you'd be coming, she thought. *They knew.*

Her hand went inside her jacket, but almost instantaneously, the men in the tavern all pulled guns. Everyone sat at the captain's table suddenly produced a weapon.

Kirsten froze, took her hand out, and put both hands up

above her head. The captain laughed.

'They want to know what's going on,' he said. 'They want to know what you know. I think tonight will be a long night for you. I think tonight will . . .'

'Get down.'

It was a quiet whisper, and it was from behind. Kirsten recognised the voice and dropped to the floor. The bar was suddenly lit up by a machine gun firing bullets here, there, and everywhere. Kirsten rolled over to one side, aware she was still in the line of fire for those who pulled their guns out towards her, but there were cries and yells. She made it to the corner before looking up and saw many of the drinkers running for exits.

Kirsten pulled her own gun out and shot a few of them who were training their weapons over towards her and towards the front door. She expected to see Hudson march through. Everywhere went quiet except for the moans and groans of those who have been shot. Kirsten saw Justin Chivers step through the door.

'I've got this. I think he went out the back door.'

Kirsten ran out past Chivers, around the back of the taverna, to see a man in the dark. He had a gun, and she dived to the left as he fired. Stalking behind trees as she got near to him, she got closer and closer until, stepping out from behind one tree, she fired, hitting him in the shoulder. It was his gun arm, and the gun fell to the ground. She ran close, jumping on the man and then hauled him up before briefly checking for other weapons.

'What the hell?' said Hudson, arriving at her side. 'What the hell?'

'Gang-related trouble. Let's go,' said Kirsten, and she started dragging the man along.

He dug his heels in the ground, started shouting at her, so she hit him across the back of the head. He was bleeding, and she'd have to get cleaned up afterwards, but she picked him up, threw him over her shoulder, and began running back to the boat. As she peered past the taverna, Justin Chivers was there at the front, still holding his automatic rifle.

'Are you good?' she said.

'I'm good.'

'Meet us at Hudson's Hotel,' she said. Chivers nodded and together Kirsten and Hudson ran for their boat, the captain of the *Garabine* over her shoulder. When she jumped into the boat, telling Hudson to step on it, he powered the vessel away and back down the coast.

'I take it the hotel's not just a simple place to hide in. I take it you own most of the staff around there!'

Hudson smiled. 'It's a good job too, isn't it? This guy better be worth it.'

'Oh, he will be,' said Kirsten. 'He will be.'

Chapter 19

Kirsten sipped her rather strong coffee, resting her feet up on a table, leaning back on a chair. In the next room, she could hear Hudson at work. Justin Chivers was also present, 'supervising', to make sure that nothing untoward happened. However, Kirsten could tell that the captain of the *Garabine* was being put through his paces.

They were in the basement of the hotel Hudson had been staying at, and she realised the Americans seemed to own most of the building. There was a communications room deep down in the recesses with access heavily restricted. Kirsten and Chivers were being extended a courtesy to be down here. It was fair to Kirsten in that she'd given payback for probably screwing up some of Hudson's work.

She wasn't one for extracting information. She'd done it recently with Marcello and with Toro Devia, but that was out in the field, having to take information quickly and make snap decisions. Dispatching them both hadn't been pleasant. Yet, Kirsten was realising more and more she didn't have those earlier qualms about dispatching someone. She still needed a reason, but it seemed to require less justification these days. Kirsten felt it was the job—a gnawing effect if she stayed alive through the horrors she saw. Would she end up like Godfrey?

She'd wanted out. She'd realised how things were going and wanted out. Craig had too, and they had called it. Then that friend of his pulled her back into the Alaska job and everything happened. Craig fell apart and then, yes, her dream of getting out had fallen, too. Hadn't it?

She wondered if Macleod was across the table, how he would react. Could she have done these last two killings if he'd been standing looking at her? Her old Inspector, a man with clear morals, practically set in stone, and yet he must have known what the service got up to. Maybe not, but he must have known it would push her to her limits. Push her morally to her limits, not just physically and emotionally. She sipped more coffee.

'Well, it's a good job somebody in here does all the work.'

Kirsten snapped out of her pondering and saw Justin Chivers smiling at the door. 'Did you get anywhere?' Kirsten asked quickly.

'I've got something for you to do. Hudson's going to continue with him. He's spilling a lot about the drugs, but as regards to what we need, he's been much quieter. Hudson..., well let's just say Hudson got a name out of him. Claretta Bowman. Goldsmith apparently worked with her on one run, or at least gave her instruction. At least according to the *Garabine's* captain.'

'You think it's real? You think it's . . .'

'I doubt he was really going to say anything else. I don't know. It's not the methods I would've used. I'm afraid these days extracting information has become something different. I always think you should do it more psychologically, not physically. But you need to go to her flat. I've got people already looking.'

'What do you mean looking?'

'They're not in the flat, just in the surrounding area. I called it through a few minutes ago just to get the perimeter set up. See if she's about. We'll get you back into Montevideo and let's see what you can dig up.'

'You look worried,' Kirsten said.

'The captain said something big was going down. Claretta was boasting, boasting about the reach Goldsmith had, boasting about how there'd be a payback. I think her father was in the Falklands. At least that's the impression that the captain took from her. It seems she has a genuine reason to hate the British.'

'I thought the Argentine hierarchy took the blame for that,' said Kirsten.

'When it's your family that is dead, many people are to blame. We killed him at the end of the day.'

'It was war.'

'War it may have been,' said Justin, 'but it doesn't matter, does it? The Russians would've killed Craig in a war. That's what we fight. You wouldn't have seen it that way.' Kirsten gave a wry smile, but Justin was deadly serious. 'You need to search the flat,' he said, 'see if you can come up with anything, any links to Goldberg or the UK.'

* * *

Kirsten lay in the boot of a car as it drove back to the embassy. Once there, she was able to step into a car that was pretending to be a taxi. She was garbed in a leather jacket with much lock-pick equipment, two guns tucked inside, knives down her trousers. She was expecting trouble, mainly because of the way Justin had been speaking. He was usually light-hearted, but now he was deadly serious.

She knew he was fond of her. Not in any sexual way, but as a colleague, someone she'd worked with and got to know. He was always good in this game, and she was glad he was here. Glad there was a friendly face she could look to. Hudson, at the end of the day, worked for someone else entirely. Then again, things had worked to their mutual benefit. If they hadn't, no doubt he would've been very different.

The flat in Montevideo was in a residential area and sat on the third floor of the block. It wasn't a high-rise block but was at least built within the last ten years. In terms of Uruguay, it was probably worth a bit, and Kirsten could see that the curtains were pulled apart, offering a view into the flat. It was probably a tactic by Bowman, so that if she was to go in and search, Kirsten would have to do most of it either on her belly or away from the window.

On arrival, she scouted three blocks around the flat and picked up at least five embassy staff watching. They weren't particularly obvious, but they were obvious to a trained eye like her. She attached an earpiece. 'Justin, you probably want to withdraw these guys.'

'They're there for your protection, in case she sees you on her return. We don't want her walking in on you. At the end of the day, if we have to kill her within her flat or trap her there, that works for me.'

'I'm not comfortable with it,' said Kirsten.

'Not your call, I'm afraid,' said Justin. 'Trust me on this.'

Kirsten didn't. But better to get on with the job and get it done quickly. Kirsten approached the set of flats and waited for a fellow resident to arrive. She held in her hand a package addressed to Claretta Bowman. The fellow resident, an occupant of a lower flat, let Kirsten in.

She climbed the steps up to the front door of the flat. Kirsten took out her lock picks and then saw an electronic device running across the top of the door. She traced it and decided she'd need to cut the power in the building, or at least on the top floor. Kirsten followed the wiring until she found a fuse box and then quietly tripped the top floor. At least, she hoped it was. It was all written in Spanish.

Nobody came running out of any of the other flats, and the other flat on the top floor remained quiet. She'd either got it right or she had tripped the wrong floor. Kirsten approached the door again, broke the lock, and entered.

Inside, she found a stylish home. The flat was open plan, and she could see the windows on the far side and the ability to look up and in from the street. Kirsten dropped to the floor.

She crawled round, opening cupboards, checking the contents, and then crawled over to the kitchen. It was small but standard, and she found a bedroom through the back and a bathroom. The second bedroom had been set up as an office. Here, Kirsten was hidden from the windows, so she thoroughly rifled through the room, reading whatever she could find. There was nothing. She crawled back through to the living room, slowly and painstakingly. She worked through every cupboard, but there was nothing, nothing at all that indicated anything to do with Goldsmith or even the UK.

'What's your status?' asked Justin.

'I've been through the place. Can't see anything.'

'Then come out,' said Justin. 'She's bound to return at some point.'

'No, got to be something. If this is who she is, she'll

have a safe somewhere in here or somewhere to drop stuff, somewhere where she can hide anything she needs—weapons, money, whatever.'

'Unless she hides it somewhere else.'

'Do you?' asked Kirsten.

'I'm not answering that one,' he said with a laugh.

Kirsten went back to work, poking here, there, and everywhere until she entered the bathroom. She stood staring at each fixture, at the cupboard above the sink, at the toilet, and then at the bath. The bath was curved at the rear. It came out very flat from the wall and then took a large bend.

Fancy. Kirsten looked at it and wondered why anyone would want this. Yes, you could lean against it. Certainly, better support to sit up, right, but then she looked at the fixture around the bath in a basic cladding that dropped around the edges. A white plastic panel went to the floor, was sealed at the corner by a joining piece that ran down between the two bits of plastic that then formed an edge.

She ran her hands across the plastic carefully and there it was. There was the edge. It was sitting in the middle of a white plastic sheet, so fine a cut that she couldn't see it. In fact, Kirsten could barely feel it. She moved left of it and tried to push, but nothing would move. All she had was solid plastic in front of her.

The dropdown edge from the lip of the bath. She ran her hands all the way to the corner where there were four bolts attractively finished with rounded tops. Four bolts that held the plastic to what must have been a wooden frame underneath.

'Somehow it's got to open,' she said to herself. Somehow. She pressed the bottom bolt. Nothing. Then the top one, nothing. What would connect then? What would hold the plastic sheet onto this side of the frame? *Of course, unless they aren't*, she thought as she pushed the bolt on the other side. It was spring-loaded, and it made a click.

Suddenly, the small panel in front of her flipped backwards. Kirsten reached into the dark beneath. Her hands went across a gun and then a piece of paper. It had an address on it. She didn't recognise the address, but it ended with a greater London postcode. She had operated in Scotland until she'd gone further afield. The idea that she wouldn't know somewhere in London didn't surprise her, but others might.

Quickly, she memorised the address. She reached in further and found another piece of paper. On it were some simple words, but it made little sense. 'Zippy does the light fade in the morning?'

'Kilo, she's coming back. She's been spotted.'

'Tidying up then. I'll be out in about three minutes.'

'She's still at least five or six out.'

'That'll be plenty,' said Kirsten.

She replaced the items into the hole behind the bath and pulled the cover back towards her.

'Made, we've been made,' said Justin suddenly.

'Extracting,' said Kirsten. 'Is she approaching? Has she gone away?'

'She's taking her phone and dialling.'

Kirsten heard something. Something in the flat was whirring. She then heard a Spanish word, 'Armado!'

Kirsten repeated it to Chivers. 'What's that word?'

'Get out,' shouted Chivers. 'Get out now. Bomb!'

Kirsten jumped to her feet, ran out of the bathroom, racing towards the door. She flung it open and jumped down to the steps that led down towards the bottom floor. As she reached the end of the first flight, a loud explosion rocked the building. She dived out of the way as the ceiling collapsed around her. She continued to tumble down.

The building shook, her ears ringing from the sound of the explosion. Kirsten felt disorientated but saw the glass windows in front of her. She was a floor up, but all around her, the building was crumbling. She took her gun, fired at the window, the glass shattering, and then she jumped through it.

There was a car below, parked along the edge of the pavement, and Kirsten fell, burying her shoulder into the roof of it. She reeled off the bonnet as a car screeched to a halt; the building collapsing. Dust spreading, sirens were blaring as Kirsten ran off. Her shoulder ached. One arm hung limp, but she knew she had to keep going. She couldn't be found there.

Kirsten tore around the corner, and a car sped up beside her, the door flying open. 'Get the hell in,' said Chivers suddenly. 'Get the hell in!' With the door closed, he raced off through the city.

'Did you get her?' said Kirsten.

'No,' he said.

'We need to find her, find her location. She wrote her location down; hidden away in London and a password, I think.'

She sat back in the seat as Justin continued to drive, throwing the car here and there before suddenly reducing to a sedate pace. Kirsten clutched her shoulder. 'This is going to hurt for a while.' She went to raise her arm up but struggled with the pain.

'Armado, that's the Spanish word for bomb,' said Justin. 'You really got to improve on your language skills.'

'I told you we shouldn't have put people out front. She'd have come in, and I'd have dealt with her when she came into the room.'

'That's why you used to be the boss,' said Chivers, smiling. 'At least you're all right.' His face became more serious now.

'No time to think about that. We've got to catch Claretta Bowman. Get this address back to the embassy. See if anyone can pick up anything on the UK side.'

'I give you this,' said Justin suddenly. 'You go to another country. You make sure it gets plenty of entertainment.'

Chapter 20

Kirsten was sitting at a table deep in the embassy, with Justin Chivers looking on. There was a military doctor looking at her shoulder, asking her to move her arm this way and that way. It was interrupting the conversation she was having with Chivers.

'The thing is,' said Kirsten, 'She's got to get out. Does she go over land or does she—Ah!'

'I take it that hurts,' said the doctor.

'Just a bit,' said Kirsten.

'I don't think she'll go overland. I'm not sure where she'll go either. Will she go to the UK?' asked Chivers.

'We've got the address; we've got the password. At some point, she's looking to meet Goldsmith, isn't she?' said Kirsten.

'I'm not sure,' said Justin. 'I'm really not sure.'

'We've got to find her. I take it we're having—Ah!' yelped Kirsten. 'It hurts in that direction as well.'

The doctor simply nodded and then pressed around her shoulder.

'We've got people everywhere. I've advised the Ambassador. We're pulling whatever resources we can. Looking into airfields; looking into borders.'

'Would she have run back across to Argentina?' asked Kirsten.

'Nothing to say that she was based there. She lived here. She may have had somewhere over there, but I don't think so. I think she's just a courier for the messages. She's not the leak. If she had somewhere over there, it wouldn't have been overt.'

Kirsten sighed. They were close. If they could get this woman, they'd understand what was going on. Clearly, there was some sort of target in the UK. XXYHD3, or 'Boom,' was on the move.

'You know what really—Ah!' said Kirsten.

'Sorry,' said the doctor, 'I just need to . . .'

'Just do whatever,' said Kirsten offhand, and then apologised to the doctor.

'Boom is on its way,' said Justin. 'It's got to be Boom, but for who and where? I feel we're on the edge of this. Just on the edge, like you can see something's going to happen, but we don't know enough.'

'That's why we need to get her. That's why—Ah! Just take it off. The whole darn thing hurts,' she said to the doctor.

The door opened and Susan Dandridge walked in.

'I've spoken to the PM, and I've spoken to Godfrey,' she said. 'We're pulling every resource we can. The potential risk here is very high.'

'Then we need to go on a hunt,' said Kirsten. She turned to the doctor. 'I'm fine.'

But the doctor turned to Dandridge. 'She's not fine. She's got a severely bruised shoulder. Luckily, there's nothing broken, but realistically, she should take it easy for the next two weeks at least.'

'It's fine,' said Kirsten.

'If I may,' said the doctor. 'Can you lift your top up? Take it off so the Ambassador can see the damage for herself.'

Out of modesty, Justin turned his back. This really made Kirsten laugh because the man wouldn't have been interested. She hauled her T-shirt off, wincing as she did so. Her entire shoulder and halfway down her arm were a deep purple. The bruising was severe.

'That's understood, doctor,' said Dandridge. 'Have you got any more to do?'

'No,' he said. 'My prescription would be rest. She's not currently fit to work, but she's going to.'

Kirsten hauled her T-shirt back on. 'Damn right.'

The doctor left, and once the door was closed, Dandridge looked at Kirsten seriously. 'It was important to have you assessed in case anything was broken. You needed to know your potential weakness. Sometimes things are there that you don't realise.'

'I know why. Let's just get out,' said Kirsten.

'Nothings come up on the borders. I spoke to Hudson, our American friend. There's been no movement among the fishing community, so I doubt she is using any backtrack to Argentina. She's been exposed here. She doesn't know how badly, so I think she'll flee,' said Dandridge. 'I think she'll flee in a big way. So, I've alerted our neighbouring embassies, alerted all stations within South America, but I think she'll go further. I think she'll head for the UK, so I've got lots of people deployed to the airports looking at commercial flights. I'm also looking at private flights.'

'And?' said Kirsten.

'Nobody's left yet either under her name or with her face. Here's a photo of her for you, Kirsten. I've pulled every asset on this,' said Dandridge. 'The station officer here has hauled in favours from not just the Americans, but our European counterparts as well. We've shared a little with them. They're worried too. It might start with us, but it could end with them too.'

'I'm going to head out,' said Kirsten, 'to see if there's anything unusual. I won't do any good here being a field person.'

'That is true,' said Justin. 'I can assist if you need, Ambassador, as I'm good at the keyboard. The best trawler you ever saw on a keyboard.'

'I've got plenty of people for that. Go ahead with Miss Stewart,' said the Ambassador. 'See if you guys can think something up. Other than that, we're in a wait-and-see situation.'

Kirsten left the embassy in a car with Justin Chivers. He drove to Carrasco airport to the north of the city. The airport pulled about two million passengers a year, and would be a good crowd to get lost in.

Arriving at the airfield, Kirsten could see the large passenger terminals. They spent the next couple of hours walking around, looking for faces, anything unusual. Kirsten could spot those from her own country and from other allies, scanning the passengers as they moved back and forth. It was a thankless task, but in fairness to the Ambassador and the station officer, they had done their job.

'We're dead space here. There's no point in us doubling up what people are doing. Where else can you take off around here?'

'You can't get a jet into anywhere else.'

'What about other airfields? If you're going to go incognito, why fly direct to the UK? Why fly to any European airport?

You're going to go through and get scanned. There might be other places you could get an aircraft out from, somewhere you could book a flight.'

'If you're going to fly, though,' said Justin, 'you have to have a flight plan. Book a flight plan in. We've scanned all those, there's nothing. Every one of those flights checks out.'

'If you can file a flight plan in the air or if you can get an aircraft into somewhere else, you could book a flight out of a different country,' said Kirsten.

'The system will think that you've been in another country. If you flew to that country on a flight plan and then flew into Uruguay without a flight plan and back from Uruguay, again with no flight plan, you'd be taking off from the other country.'

'Exactly,' said Kirsten. 'That's how I'd do it, fly low. In something that wouldn't pick up on radar easily.'

'You're talking about a small plane.'

'A plane that can set down,' said Kirsten, 'on a very short runway, but can fly to the UK.'

'You will not do the trip in one go, will you?' said Justin. 'There has to be proper jet to get all the way over there, or a heavily loaded up aircraft like a Hercules with extra fuel or something.'

'No,' said Kirsten. 'Not that way. Go up north. Go up by the Artic.'

Justin turned to her. 'Buy two coffees. Get a table over there.'

Kirsten looked blankly at him, but he just pointed. She walked over for the coffees, but turned and saw him disappearing into a shop. By the time she had been served the coffee, Justin was already sitting at the table with a map open. It showed Montevideo and the surrounding area.

'What are you doing?' she asked.

'Landing sites. Looking for landing sites. Where could we put down a small twin aircraft, a short hopper?'

'I don't know,' she said. She looked at the map. Justin began ringing areas.

'Are you sure about that?' said Kirsten. 'It doesn't look like it's even.'

'I'm not sure about anything,' he said. 'We're going to have to examine them visually.'

Kirsten watched as the man tore across the map. He ringed several areas, six in total.

'Well, that one's out,' said Kirsten. 'Too open, too exposed. People could see you if you're running around. This one here, not happening. You're going to need somewhere for the aircraft to set down on the ground. Look at it, it's marsh. These are heavy things, aircraft.'

'I'm on the hoof here,' said Justin suddenly.

'I wasn't being testy,' said Kirsten. 'But those two, no three, they're possibilities.'

Justin grabbed his coffee and drunk it in one go.

'I got a paper cup,' said Kirsten, 'as I reckoned we'd be on the move.'

Two minutes later, they were racing out of the country's major airport and driving out of the city and into the country-side. Justin always thought areas here looked like shrubbery. Burnt versions of some Scottish countryside, as if much of the vegetation just didn't bother. It took Justin only ten minutes to arrive at the first site. He got out on foot—Kirsten too—and they scoured the area for the next ten minutes.

'Nobody here,' she said. 'Next one!'

At the second site, Kirsten saw what would be a rather difficult landing. There were trees at either end, and you'd have to get the aircraft up quickly. But the area was so out of the way, and they had taken a track to get here. The pilot would have to be skilled, very skilled, but the location was very remote.

'I can't see anything, Justin. There's no sign, there's no fuel, there's nothing.' Together, they walked back to the car and drove off. As the road went up, Kirsten looked back through some trees at the area they'd been scanning. It was indeed small, and it did . . .

'Stop the car,' said Kirsten. Justin hit the brakes and nearly put her through the front windscreen.

'What?' he said.

'Look, look down on that area.' There on the ground were little black marks. A landing strip had been marked out.

Justin turned the car around and drove back down.

'She's got to be here,' he said. 'We apprehend her now before the aircraft arrives'.

'No,' said Kirsten. He looked across at her. 'Don't you see, Justin? What have we got? Nothing. We could take Bowman, and what happens? She'll probably not give anything up, or else we'll be two weeks behind while we're trying to crack her. We get the aircraft, and we get the pilot, we know where she's going. We know that route. I say we follow it. We need to infiltrate, not simply blunder our way in.'

Justin pulled the car over, hiding it off the road, and together the pair ran down the steep side that approached the open area amongst the trees.

Kirsten sat down on her haunches, looking down at the strip, and she could hear in the distance the sound of an aircraft engine. A compact figure moved down below. A blonde-haired woman wearing a rather long coat was waving up at the aircraft.

'Let's go,' said Kirsten, and tore off down through the shrubbery and the trees. The aircraft was just touching down as she reached the edge of the makeshift runway and Kirsten ran out towards it. Justin was hot on her heels.

'They'll get airborne again. They'll turn and get airborne again.'

'No, they won't,' said Kirsten. 'The wind he needs the wind to get up there. He can't run with the wind behind him.'

It was more than a slight breeze and Kirsten was proved right as the aircraft swung round and backtracked along the runway again. The pilot saw them, but didn't alter his course, tracking back down the runway.

Kirsten ran towards the aircraft and the door on the side of the aircraft opened. One shot after another was fired at her, but she weaved and ran close behind the aircraft, shooting her gun just over the top. Claudia Bowman, she presumed, had been firing at her, and she now ducked back inside.

The aircraft was slowing to turn around. Kirsten approached the door. Bowman popped her head out to shoot, and Kirsten caught her with a fist to the face. She stepped inside and Bowman could shove Kirsten's shoulder, catching the inside of the door.

Kirsten yelped, but as Bowman went to jump on her, Kirsten caught her with a kick to the stomach, then one to the head. Then she ran through to the cockpit, bursting through the cabin door as the man turned around with a gun. She grabbed his wrist, wrenching it hard. Clearly, the man was just a pilot, and he simply dropped the gun.

Kirsten grabbed him by the throat. 'Stop the damn engines,' she said. 'Stop them now.' A voice behind her said, 'No.' The noise inside the aircraft was loud and they were having to make themselves shout to be heard.

'We go,' said Justin. 'Find out where they were going and we go.' Kirsten looked over her shoulder and Bowman was lying on the ground out cold.

'Do you know how to fly?' asked Kirsten.

'Well, pretty well.'

Justin Chivers strolled through and grabbed the pilot's board.

'I can follow that,' he said. He pushed it to one side. 'Of course, we've got to get out of here first.' Justin pulled out his gun and held it to the pilot's head. 'If you get us out of here, you'll live. If you don't, you'll die. Either way, in the next ten minutes, we're going to be up in that sky heading to your destination. If we're not, you won't be going anywhere.'

'Do you know her?' asked Kirsten, pointing at Bowman behind her.

'No,' said the pilot, 'I just fly.' Kirsten thought he was German by the accent, certainly European.

'Then fly you shall. I'll stuff myself in the back and close the door,' said Kirsten. 'Best if you give him a hand, Justin.'

Kirsten went into the rear of the aircraft and secured Bowman. She would search her in due course. There'd be plenty to do en route, for they'd have to contact someone to pick the pilot and Bowman up. But for now, it was time to get underway.

Chapter 21

The aircraft flew low over the trees as it routed north out of Uruguay. Back in Uruguay, searches would still go on for Claretta Bowman. Maybe the aircraft would be traced from above by satellite; who could tell? That was difficult to do, as the pilot remained so low. It ate up the aircraft's fuel, but it afforded terrific secrecy.

The pilot's plan was initially a quick hop into Argentina. From there, he had a flight plan ready, and he would start the journey north up through South America, North America, and across to Iceland. Then south, eventually arriving in London three days later.

Kirsten was left alone in the rear with Claretta Bowman. The woman looked scared, and when Kirsten searched her, she found a scrap of paper detailing a hotel somewhere just outside London. Again, Kirsten wasn't familiar with the location, but someone would be back in London.

When they stopped that evening up in Florida, Kirsten attended the booked hotel, along with the pilot, leaving Chivers on the plane with Bowman. During the flight, the pilot had decided that he would assist in all ways. Having talked to him, Justin believed the man was simply a pilot ferrying a passenger. The man knew Claretta was probably on the run from someone, but he was happy to assist because of the amount of money he would get for the trip. Now, he was just happy to complete the trip, undergo some questioning, and hopefully walk free.

When they got to their small hotel room beside the tiny airfield in Florida, Kirsten took out her gun and put it in the man's back.

'You'll stay in your hotel room tonight. Sleep. You'll contact no one because if you do, you won't wake up. When you get to the end of our trip and drop us off in London, you'll meet a friend of mine. They'll make sure you have got nothing to do with what's going on with the woman in the rear of the plane. Hopefully, you'll be able to fly off somewhere else.'

Kirsten called in the details she found on Claretta Bowman, and a short time later, received a message to pop out to a diner along the way. Kirsten took a taxi and sat down in what she thought looked like the classic American diner. There was reddish-purple seating in a long row, and opposite was a serving bar. Behind it, food was being prepared.

A waitress came and took her order and Kirsten took the opportunity to have scrambled eggs and bacon, along with pancakes. That it was eleven o'clock at night didn't seem to bother anyone. *One up for capitalism*, she thought.

As Kirsten started eating, a man approached and asked if he could sit opposite. He was wearing a large blue shirt, dark slacks, and had his hair slicked back. He must have been in his early fifties and she asked him how his Uncle Tom was. Tom apparently was fine, although the gallbladder was still giving him gyp.

'You must be . . .?'

'I'm Alan Jones, station officer. Well, you've led everyone on a merry dance back in Uruguay. Dandridge is annoyed you didn't call her sooner. She was having the place searched like crazy.'

'Has she stopped?'

'No. Godfrey told her to keep going for the next day or two. Make it look like we were still hunting.'

'Good. I plan to continue the trip Bowman would have made. Our pilot has been very cooperative. I don't believe he's involved, but when we get to London, Godfrey can find that out himself. As it is, he's going to fly us. We'll keep going on this timescale and when we get there, I'll go to the hotel. Either that or I'll keep Bowman. We'll see if she breaks on the flight.'

'Godfrey says you're to infiltrate. However you do it, get in underneath and find out what's going on. You're to act with extreme prejudice against anyone threatening the United Kingdom. Don't hold back. He's worried.'

'He should be worried. XXYHD3 on the move. Boom.'

'You do realise,' said Alan, 'that the police back in Uruguay are wondering how a bomb that size was brought into the building in Montevideo. All the flats were destroyed. A couple of casualties went with it.'

Kirsten nodded and bit her tongue. On previous occasions she had been involved with such fatalities she had a reaction of disgust, but to be honest, now she just seemed to go with it. That worried her. Those were innocent people that died, all from a bad judgment call. *Justin handled that*, she thought. She would not dump him in it before Alan.

'Maybe she used a bit. Maybe.'

'If she did, she's crazy,' said Alan. 'Anyway, somebody will wait for you in London. In the meantime, is there anything else I can do for you?'

'Passport?'

He handed her a small envelope containing passports for her and Chivers. When they had landed in Florida, no one had batted an eyelid, even though they should have. It was smoothly done.

Kirsten returned to the plane the next morning, and the pilot set off on the long haul towards Iceland. They stopped there for the night and Kirsten would spend most of the day in the aircraft's rear. Bowman cried a lot.

'You don't think he'll defend you then?' asked Kirsten. 'We can. We can look after you, but I need to know what's going on.'

'You don't get it, do you? He'll kill me.'

'Not if I kill him first,' said Kirsten. 'What's going on? Why is . . .'

'Don't,' she said. 'Don't ask.'

'XXYHD3.' Bowman looked blankly at Kirsten. 'Boom,' she said, and suddenly there was a brief reaction on the woman's face. She tried to control it, but clearly, it had shocked her. 'You tried to blow me up with some of it when I was in your flat.'

'Well, that's what you get for . . .'

Kirsten smacked the woman with the back of her hand. 'You tried to blow me up. Don't act as if you're in charge here. Try to act as if you've not got any way out. It's either me or it's Goldsmith, and if you don't talk to me, I'll dump you in London for him.' The woman's eyes suddenly went wide. Fear shot through her.

'You can't. You can't leave me with him. He won't just, you

174

know, kill me; he'll . . .'

'He'll make an example of you. Rip you to shreds. He will make it the most painful time of your life before he ends you,' said Kirsten. She didn't even know who Goldsmith was, but she was going to play up on the woman's fears.

'If I tell you, what can you . . .'

'I can guarantee you nothing except that he won't get hold of you.'

Kirsten wondered if Godfrey would be any more lenient. Who knew what Godfrey would do to extract information or how? He had limits. Well, he had visible limits. In the shadows, though, who knew what Godfrey did?

'Okay,' said the woman. 'Okay, I will come with you.'

'No, no, no. You've got to earn that right,' said Kirsten. 'You see, between now and London, I need to know everything you know about your interaction with Goldsmith. I need to know what's going on. I need to know where and when. You've done more than keep a little of that explosive in your building.'

'You don't understand what he's like; he's . . .'

'He's what? Have you met him?' asked Kirsten.

'No, never.'

'Has he met you?'

'How do you mean?'

'Have you ever suspected anybody might be Goldsmith talking to you?'

'No one spoke to me. I operated solely on dropped messages. He keeps a defensive ring around himself.'

'So, what are you to do in London, then?'

'He said we were all to meet at the hotel. At the hotel, we will get instructions. I supplied some of the explosive, so I must set one device off. It was about bringing us all in together. We have all come from different places, I think.'

'You what?' blurted Kirsten. 'Different places? You mean this explosive has been brought in from somewhere else?'

'Yes,' she said, 'they've brought it in small doses. It doesn't need to be too big. You saw what it did to the flat. That was so small. I wired that up myself. Took a piece. He said I could do it. I messaged and said I needed to protect the information. He told me not to be afraid to blow myself up if it all went that way.'

'Yes, that's harder to do than just say, isn't it? Especially when it comes down to it. Especially when you're the one at the end of that bomb. So, you're to meet?' said Kirsten. 'You're to meet, and then he'll do what?'

'He'll tell us where to go and how to set off the bombs. We don't know where they're being set off, we just know it's the UK, England.'

'You know who the target is?'

'No. All I know is that the people coming to do this must not like your country. That's how he sold it to me. My father was killed by your people in the Falklands.'

'And the others, will they be similar?'

'I only suspect,' she said, 'as I've never met them. Everything that we did, the information running out of the Argentinian embassy, I never got to see who it was. We had a drop arrangement set up by him. Goldsmith set it all up. I only contacted the boat people, the fishermen that ran me back and forward. I had another contact then to drop the information to. They sent it to England. Or at least they forwarded it to somewhere. Lots of chains that can be broken without reaching him. He's not stupid. He's been years setting this up, working in the dark, quietly, but this, this is what he wants.'

'And does he know you? Do you think he knows what you look like?'

'I don't know. He said that the password would identify us. I don't know if he even wants to know what we look like. In case he saw it, in case he was . . .'

Kirsten sat down for a moment. *In case your face was put in front of him*, she thought. *In case at some point you were photographed, or you came in front of . . . When would his expression have to be controlled? Could he be surprised? When would . . .*

It dawned on Kirsten this might be somebody on the inside. This could be somebody within the organisation. Somebody in the service could actually work out where all the important targets were. They'd know what information was needed, could have it fed to certain places without seeing it themselves. They would be kept apart from it.

If they were based in the UK, but the information came from other parts of the world, they would be in the clear. They'd have to understand the system and manipulate it, see the red herrings being put in. Knowing who would know who had details of important movements. They could get people to break in, to use their codes. They would know people within the service, an inside job. An inside job so tight that they never actually knew what anybody looked like, so if anyone who stood in front of them, their first question would be 'Who is that?'

They run it so dark they don't even know what the people they're working with look like. Kirsten felt afraid. Someone who could act so deep, who could control themselves so well that they wouldn't risk even the slightest flicker of a face when glancing at some of their minions, would really have attention to detail and planning.

She would have to infiltrate. There was no choice now. She would have to be Bowman, have to be part of whatever was going on and break it up from there. She lay back in the plane's seat. One stop in Iceland, the next, London.

It was late when they arrived in London, landing at eight o'clock at night. The pilot scheduled the plane to depart off to Germany the next day, and they'd keep that running. After all, they didn't want him to be seen as stepping away from his normal routine.

The aircraft was hangered that night and when it was taken inside, a car pulled up and Claretta Bowman was taken away by Godfrey. Kirsten had questioned her all the way from Iceland that day, building up a cover story, making sure she understood what Bowman had done. It would be a test to impersonate her.

The pilot disappeared off to a hotel. The following day, when he stepped on board the plane, one of Godfrey's people was there with him. On the flight back to Germany, they would make sure that he was exactly who he said he was.

Kirsten made for the hotel in London that Bowman had booked, checked in, and slept there that night. Some clothing had arrived mysteriously in her wardrobe, and she sat preparing for a meeting the next day. This was it. This is what it had all been about, and what she'd worked towards. Something was afoot, and tomorrow she'd hopefully find out exactly what.

Chapter 22

Kirsten rose the next morning and showered, feeling some trepidation in her stomach. This was it. This was the day when she'd either end up dead or understand what was going on. She felt like she was walking in blind. Yes, she'd spent hours with Claretta Bowman. She understood the woman, could give a history of her, was able to say what she'd done. She had her password to confirm who she was, but would Goldsmith even be there?

Kirsten may also have to plant a bomb. How would this work? What sort of devious mind would this man have? When she was there, did she simply walk in and shoot everyone? Bowman had said that Kirsten was not to approach with a gun or any other weapon. Kirsten was thankful that her martial arts training meant that she was a weapon in herself, but even so, she was about to walk into the dragon's den with the dragon fully awake.

She breakfasted that day on her favourite, scrambled eggs, bacon, and a little dollop of maple syrup on top before ordering a taxi. She sat for the forty minutes that it took for the taxi to approach a house in the north of London. A solitary man in the house told her to step outside to the taxi at the rear of the house. It swept her away and deposited her in the country at a farm.

When she exited, she carried no bags and walked down a long driveway that led to a large cottage. When she reached the door of the cottage, she rapped a large knocker and stood back, awaiting her fate. Inside, she was shaking. If they were looking for Bowman, they could open the door and simply blow her away. But if they didn't know what Bowman looked like, if the deceit had been run the way Kirsten thought it had, then she may just get away with it.

The door opened, and a man stood there looking her up and down.

'And you are?'

'Claretta Bowman,' said Kirsten.

'How long have you lived in Argentina?'

'All my life, but I have worked in many European establishments there, trained to work with their diplomats and other people so I can take on the accent. There was a Scottish woman that I worked with. I learnt to do this soft highland Scottish accent. Not the usual Glasgow one, you hear.'

There had been a Scottish woman working with Claretta Bowman in her past, but Bowman had never picked up the accent.

The man put his hand out. 'Welcome, Mrs Bowman.'

'Miss,' said Kirsten directly.

'Apologies,' Miss Bowman. 'It was a test. I take it you're here for vengeance. Here for your father and your brother. '

'I don't have a brother,' said Kirsten, 'but yes, I am here for my father.'

'He died in the Falklands. Which regimen was it? The fifth.'

'The third,' said Kirsten instantly. 'Are we done with all the questions? I don't find the concern particularly sincere.'

'We're all here for our own reasons, with one common enemy. I'm Michael Goldsmith. Your mobile, please.'

The man was short, with thick, black-rimmed glasses. Kirsten thought he looked like a civil servant from the middle of London. He was certainly old, possibly sixty, going on for seventy, although he wasn't out of shape. Goldsmith wore a plain tie on a white shirt that maybe spoke about the generation he came from, and he welcomed her inside.

The farmhouse looked just like an everyday farmhouse. Crockery set up in a large kitchen in which burned a fire with a griddle pan arrangement. Kirsten was shown to her room on the first floor. It was small with a single bed, and she was asked to wait here, advised that everyone was arriving within half an hour of each other. Soon they would all be here and find out about the plan.

Kirsten watched from her window, but it faced the wrong way, and she didn't see anyone arrive at the house, although she heard them. She waited in her room wondering how long it would be, before finally a knock came, and the door opened to reveal Goldsmith.

'If you'll come downstairs to the kitchen,' he said, 'I have some soup on. We shall eat and then we shall discuss what we will do.'

The man was very matter-of-fact, and Kirsten struggled to imagine him as a killer. Everything he did was so simple, so straightforward. He was almost charming.

The soup was tomato with basil, and it was quite excellent. Kirsten couldn't taste anything in it that shouldn't have been there. There were no after-effects. Once lunch was concluded with a serving of bread, Goldsmith ushered everyone into the next room. There on a wall was a map of London. Goldsmith made everyone sit down and stood at the front and took his jacket off. His tie swung loose from his collar, and he gave a grin as he welcomed everyone.

'We are here for different reasons, and while we are here, there are no names to be used amongst you. You all know me as Goldsmith. I have worked hard over the years to set this up, worked hard to bring down those that oppress my country. Those who use methods not in keeping with British methods.

'We are no longer gentlemen and gentlewomen in this land. We have partners who do such horrid things. My land is ruined by people who will let anything go. Politicians who will accept any change just so long as they get elected for the next five years. Everything is slipping, and so it is time to show people what happens to a country with no backbone, how simple it is for others to come and cause panic and terror.

'There are others available afterwards who will pick up the mess politically, who will cause a change. I thank you all for coming, for you have a hate for my country. You have a desire to see it punished for past transgressions against you. We may differ on that, but our means will certainly be the same to different ends. Please, can I ask that you take one chain laid on the table at the side and attach it around your neck? It's a reasonably tight fit, but it won't choke you.'

Kirsten stood with the rest. There were eight of them, three women and five men. The men and women were from differing ethnic backgrounds, two black, two Asian. Another one that looked possibly Middle Eastern, as well as one who could have been from the South Seas. Another was distinctly American.

Kirsten took the chain and then attached it round her neck.

There was a small heart shape in the middle of the chain and Kirsten saw it wouldn't come off.

Once everyone had put the chains around them, Goldsmith asked them to sit down again, and he then produced a flip chart with a drawing of the chain on it.

'You have put on the chain now and it is quite unbreakable. The only way to remove that chain would be with a special laser cutter that I don't have here. Before anybody thinks of trying, inside each of your necklaces in the heart, is a little dose of XXYHD 3. You're all carrying boom with you. You may say this is a bit risky, but it's fine, it won't go off. It's secured inside, unless it receives a signal from me, at which point it will explode and you will cease to exist.

'This is to make sure that no one backs out of our plan. You will all carry with you a case tomorrow. The case will be attached to you, and one of those cases will contain a bomb. You will be told where to go on the map, randomly assigned to any of these targets. You will go to London from here. Then kill some time in London walking around, and then, at the appropriate time, you will make your way to these places. When you're in these places, the chain to your wrists and the case will become detached and you will set the case down and you will leave.

'You will run away from London as fast as you can to wherever you can. The chain around your neck will be deactivated, so you may get a laser cutter to cut that chain, and you will have some XXYHD 3 with you. You can trade it on the black market, and it'll bring you some money. It's my thank you for a job well done. We will never see each other again. You will know you have done your part in causing one of the worst disasters to befall London and the UK in its history.'

Kirsten could see the others fidgeting around her, but Goldsmith calmed them down.

'Just to make sure we stay focused, I realise you're a little upset, but you must have known my methods by now. Wherever I have worked out in the field, I accepted nothing except the best in the information supplied, and if it didn't, I cut ties. I cut ties rather abruptly, so forgive me if I say I told you so. At least I thought I did it in a language everyone could understand.

'Tonight, you will eat together, and then you will retire to your beds. In the morning, you will get up, dressed in the clothes that I have provided upstairs, and will depart into London, individually at the appropriate times. I have detailed here for you where you should go. You may not take the paper out with you. Here, you will learn. If you're unfamiliar with London, you will sit tonight and you will study where you are to be. Anyone not in the correct place at the correct time will have their little portion of boom attached around their neck activated.

'It's no sweat off my nose. If you're carrying the briefcase that has the large quantity of boom in it, you will cause enough damage to this city of London that I will be happy with my efforts. Even if I am a little disappointed, you never got to the right place. I won't miss any of you, so make sure you do what you need to do. Understand, you're an enemy of the country.

'Your desire to afflict pain on it is what has brought you here and is why you're being used by me. I don't use people without giving them a reward. As I say, the boom in your neck, when sold on, will be more than adequate payment.'

Kirsten didn't like the sound of this. More like the boom in the neck would be used to eliminate you. He's just referred to everyone as enemies of the state. The man sees himself as a patriot, albeit a strange one. It wouldn't be unheard of that people would hurt their own country to make it better, zealots especially. *Goldsmith. Who was Michael Goldsmith?* She'd never heard of him in the service.

Kirsten sat that night looking at where she had to go. She looked at the different places people could be. Nine of them were above ground, nine of them were immediately obvious. With patience, Kirsten tried to memorise the map, tried to remember where everyone was, to keep it in her head. She also looked at the underground system that one carrier was going for.

If he blew that up, if he took the structure underneath, that would cause massive devastation. It was also close to the Houses of Parliament. It was close to Buckingham Palace, it was close to so much. Who were they going after? Who would be around?

Kirsten retired to bed that night wondering how she should play this. She knew she would get up and disappear, number four out of eight, off to the streets of London. She knew she had four hours then, four hours to get in position. Where would she go in the meantime? How could she be seen to be doing Goldsmith's will while contacting the service? He may have her monitored after all.

He said there was a small explosive inside, but maybe the necklaces would tell him where you were as well. She couldn't very well walk into the headquarters of MI5, or march into a police station. She had to look like she was doing what she was told.

Kirsten lay on the bed thinking, trying to forget she had an explosive hanging around her neck. The good side was,

Goldsmith suspected nothing. He'd accepted her as Bowman. Her deceit had worked. Her plan had worked, and she was on the inside. She had infiltrated the circle, but could she figure out a way to stop the devastation? Could she figure out a way to contact the service without being seen?

She trawled through all the locations in London she'd been briefed about when she worked for the service. Places where she could look for help and how to do it. She'd need help with this one. She needed a techy, someone who understood what to do with the necklace. Because if she was seen with anyone, if she was seen trying to make contact, then her head would quickly disappear along with most of the rest of her. She'd have to play this right. She'd have to play this right, or she'd be dead along with a lot of other people.

Chapter 23

Kirsten did not sleep well. The idea of having a small explosive around her neck was terrifying, but she knew there was no way out of it. During the small hours, when she was awake, she contemplated the fact that she may not get the chain off. She may have to warn someone and sacrifice herself to stop a worse disaster.

She knew where she was heading, knew the directions she would take once she was dropped off in London. The British Museum was a go point, a point where you could call for help and assistance. Yes, they knew the initial address that Kirsten had gone to, but having been moved, her trail was gone.

Contact with any of her people had been removed. They could try to trawl through London, check CCTV, but it would still be hard to pick her up. Very much a shot in the dark. But by going to the British Museum, she could trigger a response. She could get someone to her, but they'd have to be coy. After all, maybe Goldsmith was watching.

Next morning, she caught a taxi from the farmhouse, which dropped her at the station, and she took the train to London, as previously instructed by Goldsmith. She'd eventually be in Trafalgar Square at the appointed hour of two o'clock. As the time was only ten, Kirsten had four hours to kill, four hours to work out a solution.

She took the train across the city, then the tube out to the British Museum. It wasn't overly busy, but there were enough tourists and locals about, and she knew the risk she was taking. If anything went wrong, the surrounding people would be the ones to suffer as well as her. She was struggling not to warn them all off, grab a bell and shout, 'Unclean, plague. Keep away, keep away.'

They had taught her previously about the small case in the Egyptian Exhibit. It looked like a stone set inside a cabinet with a small button that lit up the stonework in front of them. All she had to do was press that button five times . . . and then hang about.

Kirsten smiled as she wandered around the exhibits, resisting the temptation to route straight for the button that she needed to use. She instead took her time and drifted for fifteen minutes around the Egyptian mummies and other artefacts. Then she stood in front of the cabinet with the slab inside.

Quickly, Kirsten pressed the button five times in quick succession. Then she walked off, wandered around several exhibits, and then made her way up to the cafeteria. She had a coffee before making her way back to the exhibits. She would look left and right, glancing here and there, looking for someone, anyone, to contact her.

Then she saw him. He had a large cravat on with blue trousers and a smart suit. As he walked past, he tapped her on the side almost gently, imperceptibly. It was Chivers. They walked in opposite directions, but Kirsten made her way to the suggestions box and quickly noted down her dilemma. She popped it in and walked off to the cafeteria again where she sat down, had another drink, awaiting what would happen.

She'd left in the note instruction that she had an unbreakable chain requiring a laser. She also had a bomb around her neck, and at two o'clock, she would be at Trafalgar Square, ready to detonate the case that she carried. Chivers would realise that things would not be that smooth. She was probably a guinea pig like the rest of them, Goldsmith's expendable people.

She sat with her coffee until the waitress came over and asked if she should clear it away. As she did so, she dropped a napkin on the floor. Rather than pick it up, the woman turned away with a cup of coffee, now empty of its liquid, and took it back to the kitchen area. Kirsten knelt, picked up the napkin, and opened it up.

Grosvenor Street. That would be half an hour away. Kirsten calmly stood up, walked straight out of the museum's doors and down to the nearby underground. It took twenty minutes to get across to Grosvenor street, and then she looked in shops and walking back and forward, checking down alleyways. As she walked past one, she looked down and saw a man waving at her. Instantly, she turned down it and then into what looked like a storage room of some sort. As she walked through the door, it was closed behind her. Chivers stood opposite.

'Let me see it,' he said. Kirsten walked over to him, allowing him to look at the necklace.

'No radio waves can get in here. No signals. This is a blackout room.' He studied the chain around her neck.

'Have you got anything that can cut it?' She asked.

'It's on its way. It won't be long. When it comes, I'll need you to hold up a few other things as the door opens.'

'Why?'

'To keep the signals out. To make sure. We should be all

right. I just don't know. He's going to realise you're off the grid.'

'In which case, I should go back out. Give me a signal when they arrive. We need to do this quick.'

'What else do you know?'

'I need to get back out. If he thinks the signal's gone off for too long . . .'

'He could just blow it,' said Chivers.

'He could start blowing up everybody at this point. Just screw the plan and detonate us all from wherever he is. He can detonate that bomb.'

She turned away from Chivers. Kirsten marched out of the door back into the street and calmly walked up and down, looking in at the shop windows. Someone walked past her.

'It'll be here in an hour.'

Kirsten walked off. She checked her timepiece and disappeared along Grosvenor Road and took herself on a circuitous route. If he was watching closely, Goldsmith might get perturbed. As she made her way past windows again, pretending to look at products, she was passed by, this time, by a Middle Eastern woman.

'He's ready for you,' came a quiet whisper.

Kirsten made for the alley, turned down, walked in the door, closing it behind her. In the room was now a large laser set up. Chivers pulled her over, made her kneel, and yanked the chain across. The laser was activated and quickly it cut through. As it was working its way through the chain, Chivers took the case that Kirsten was still carrying, put it up on the desk, and opened it and looked inside.

'There's no bomb,' he said to Kirsten. 'There's no bomb here.'

It was as she suspected; only one case contained a bomb.

Everything else was a decoy. Everyone else was set up to explode. She wondered just how it would work.

'I need to get back out there,' she said, but quickly she grabbed a pen and paper off of Chivers and she started writing the locations of everyone else.

'This is where they're all going, but he's also sent someone to the tube. Why are they going to the tube?'

'I don't know,' said Chivers. 'We're keeping that device in here, though.' He turned to the two other men with him.

'Don't come out. Once we're through that door, keep it shut until the box arrives to put it in.'

'The box?' asked Kirsten.

'I've got a box that'll shield it until we can work on it properly. It would stop activation. Either that or we'll take it somewhere and blow it up.'

'Good idea,' said Kirsten. 'Come on.'

'Wait,' said Justin. He handed Kirsten a mobile and a gun. He turned and watched as those with the necklace retreated to the far corner of the room. They then put more shielding around it before the pair of them could disappear out of the door.

'How long since you started cutting it?'

'Ten minutes,' said Justin. 'How long have we got until his go time?'

'I reckon we're still good. Forty minutes?' she surmised. 'Maybe more. We can probably get to everyone. Can we get any more of those boxes, something we can put the necklaces in?'

Kirsten heard an explosion.

'Dear God,' she said, 'what was that?'

Justin picked up his phone, quickly tapped a number. 'Yes,'

he said. 'Where? When?' He turned to Kirsten. 'Westminster Bridge,' he said. 'He's just set one of those necklaces off on Westminster Bridge.'

'We don't know where the other people are. They're just walking around. They could be anywhere. Westminster Bridge wasn't a final destination.'

They could hear another explosion, followed by a third one.

As much as it pained her, Kirsten turned to Justin and said, 'We need to know those locations. We need to work out . . .'

Justin returned to his mobile. There was another explosion. 'That was four!'

Kirsten stood in the middle of the street, looking at Justin.

'Think what's going on. What's going on now? He brings us in. Which one of the targets?'

'Victoria Line Underground. It's a good one,' he said. 'Go there. They can't be that far from it.'

Kirsten took off, running along the streets as hard as she could. The traffic was coming to a standstill. Panic was taking over. She saw the police close roads down. *Who would Goldsmith blow up next? Who was on the move?*

As Kirsten ran, her phone went off, and she picked it up. 'The King,' said Chivers. 'The King. He's going to be above the Victoria line, close to it. If they're holding the bomb inside that case, it'll take him out and everything else. If it is a bomb the size of that case, it could . . .'

'I know,' said Kirsten, running as hard as she could. Could she jump on a tube to get there? And if she found the Victoria Line, she still had to spot one of the bombers. She'd seen their faces; she would recognise them again, but they were in a massive crowd.

Another explosion went off. *How many was that? Five?*

Kirsten ran down steps into the Victoria Line, scanning.

She wondered how far she would be from where the king was entertaining two stops down. *Could she jump on the tube? Was the tube still moving? Would they get instruction?*

The tube staff suddenly told everyone they were closed, ushering people back up the stairs. Kirsten ran back up the steps. As she arrived at the top of them, she heard another explosion. Six.

Her phone went off again. 'Kensington Gardens, that was Kensington Gardens. We've still got one near the tube. You need to get there.' There was another explosion.

'That's another one. Kirsten, there're bodies everywhere.' She heard ambulance sirens, police sirens, all ringing through the air. People were panicking all around her, running inside the shops, desperate for a place to hide. Anywhere out in the open seemed to be the last place people wanted to be.

A seventh explosion went up. That meant there was one more. She was now only a stop away from where she needed to be. Surely this would be it. He'd be holding off watching to see where his necklace of death was. She knew that the person going couldn't get out of it. They'd have to go through with it, trust him. They were following through on the commitment they'd have to make. But could she get there?

And do what? she thought. *Do what exactly?*

She looked left and right as she approached the tube station. They were pushing everybody back. The crowds were in a panic, people pushing this way and that. Kirsten jumped on a lamppost and started climbing up, looking over the crowd. Over a hundred yards away, she saw him, a black man, and she could just about glimpse the necklace.

He was still working his way towards the tube station, still trying to get there, which made him so obvious. Kirsten began shouting at the crowd, but she had no jurisdiction. Nor did she have a loud enough voice. There were police now trying to push the crowd one way or the other, but where do they go?

London was in chaos. Panic was setting over the streets. *Where did she send them? What could she do?* Kirsten shouted over at the black man. She pulled down her top to expose her neckline, and screamed at him she could help, that the necklace wasn't there.

'Look,' she yelled, 'look! The necklace is not here.'

The necklace exploded around the neck of the black man. So powerful was the force that, over a hundred yards away, it knocked Kirsten off the lamppost. She fell into a crowd of people, her shoulder screaming at her. Bits of masonry fell off nearby walls, windows blew out. Her ears rang as she tried to pick herself back up.

That was eight, she said to herself, an intense focus amidst all the chaos that was going on around her. Everywhere she looked, people were screaming. Others lay dead. People ran as hard as they could, buffeting her here and there. Her shoulder rang with pain, and she tried to think.

That was eight. Eight explosions.

Horrific as it was, body parts strewn here, there, and everywhere, this wasn't the big thing. This wasn't the true chaos that was coming. *What had he done? What was the last piece?* Kirsten swallowed hard. He was going to do it himself. He had a reason. What was he going to do? Goldsmith had used the others. What was he really doing?

Chapter 24

Kirsten staggered around, her mind reeling. She needed to react. She needed to get going. Around her, she saw people panicking, sprinting off. Others sat down on their bottoms, exhausted. Meanwhile, some tried to tend to those who had been caught up in the blast but were still alive. Somebody was crying. Others were screaming. The place was an utter mess. *Think, Kirsten*, she said to herself. *Think*!

Her phone rang. 'Kirsten,' she answered.

'You okay?' asked Justin on the other end.

'Yes, I am, but there's no gigantic explosion.'

'No, there isn't. It means he must be . . .'

'Yes. Yes, I worked that out. He must be doing it himself. He must be planting the bomb elsewhere, but why? Why set off all these other ones? Why? It's gone crazy. Absolutely gone crazy. Where would he go, though? Where would you explode? Underground? If you set off the underground, you'd collapse a lot, wouldn't you? But where? Is it the underground near the palace? Is it the underground near?' Kirsten was blurting out now, aware that some people were watching her like she was some sort of mad conspiracy theorist.

'You need to go this way, this way, love,' said a policeman, trying to clear the area. Kirsten gave him a vague nod. She needed to get out. She needed to get somewhere with more space. Somewhere where she could think. Anywhere.

'You still there?' asked Justin. 'Where could he go? Where could he achieve the greatest impact? Most damage?'

'It's a bloody mess, Justin. The city's a mess. We've got fear and panic everywhere.'

'But he wanted a target. He wanted information about a target. He asked about very important people. He must be going after somebody important. There must be someone.'

'It could have just been a cover, a cover while he ran the explosives in.'

'But why?' asked Justin. 'Why talk to you about the large bomb? The explosives were kept quiet. And there's the information about the important person.'

'Do we know what's come through? Do we have any idea?'

'Information on the prime minister, information on the king. Information on various cabinet officials, various politicians, diary extracts, things like that.'

'Tracking their movements,' said Kirsten. *Tracking their movements, but why?* she thought. She stumbled over to the pavement and sat down on her bottom, now clear of the driving crowds trying to exit the area. 'Why?'

'I don't know,' said Justin. 'I don't know. I mean, the king, they'll get him out of here, they'll move him.'

'And the prime minister?' asked Kirsten.

'They'll take him to a secure location, a secret bunker. Pull him away until it's okay.'

'And where's that bunker?'

'I don't know,' said Justin. 'I don't get told that sort of thing. That's above my pay grade.'

'I thought you might have known.'

'No, no, no,' he said. 'Maybe Godfrey. Godfrey might know.'

'I'll ring Godfrey then,' she said, and closed their call. Kirsten rang a number and got a secretary. 'I'm afraid Godfrey's not available,' she said. 'He is rather busy at the moment.'

'It's his agent in London. He needs to talk to me.'

She was put on hold, and then twenty seconds later, 'You better have something for me. This has all gone wrong. This is all . . .'

'Shut up,' said Kirsten. 'Tell me, prime minister, the king, where are they now?'

'They'll be operating on the protocol. They'll be taken to the bunkers, taken out of the way.'

'And where's the bunker?'

'Who's? Which one?'

'Where's the king?'

'Outside London.'

'What about the prime minister?'

'Well, he's still got to be operational, so the bunker is down in London. It's basically below the new tube line. The King Arthur line. Under the Thames. The one that's been built recently.'

'But is it far from the King Arthur line?'

'No. I mean, it's deep underneath. The line passes a wee bit above it. They can get out to that line if they had to. It's an extra escape route.'

'You've got to tell them to move him. I think that's what he's going for. I think he's going for the big one. If he puts this type of bomb there, it'll . . .'

'It'll what?'

'It'll take him out, and everybody else that's in there. You need to move them.'

'He's locked down. They won't come out of there,' said Godfrey. 'I won't be able to talk to them. They'll be fearing that we're compromised. He'll want to know the reason for the bombings. He'll need concrete evidence.'

'Well, talk to him, dammit. I've got to get over there.'

King Arthur line, she thought. *The King Arthur line. What else did Godfrey say? He said it was under the Thames. I need to get there.*

Kirsten tried to work out where she was. Disorientated, she picked up her phone and activated the mapping feature. *Quickest time*, she thought. *The quickest time.*

Kirsten looked around her. She saw a police motorbike sitting on one side and ran over, jumping onto it. Kirsten then broke off some of the cover and managed to hot-wire it and got the bike going.

She went to hare off when a hand was placed on her shoulder. She turned to see a police outrider in full uniform and helmet. 'Miss, you can't do that. The roads are chock-a-bloc. You won't get anywhere.'

'I need to get to the King Arthur line. I need to get to the Thames.'

'Safest place is to go inside. Go inside and wait this out.'

'I need . . .'

'I'm telling you now; step off the bike and move inside.'

Kirsten didn't have time for this. She stepped off her bike, reached over, physically grabbed the officer and threw him against the wall. He fell hard, but she never gave him a chance before jumping onto the police bike. The throttle was still going, and she drove off at speed.

She put on the siren and flashing light, and headed as fast as she could towards the Thames and the subway entrance for the King Arthur line. As she approached several roadblocks, Kirsten was waved to turn away. But she kept going, mounting the pavement, swerving in and out, and breaking some barriers. Nothing was going to stop her. There was one chance, one chance to stop this if, of course, she was right.

But she had to be right. It all made sense now. He had used them all. After all, what were they to him? They were nothing. They were enemies of the state. Here he was trying to show an example, trying to get rid of what he thought was the problem with the country. Goldsmith, whoever he truly was, was a right raving looney, but a clever one.

Kirsten found the roads clear on the edge of the Thames. The police were either pushing people inside buildings or pushing them out of the city. She pulled up on the bike, seeing the entrance down to the new underground line and the new platforms that were awaiting. There was a steel mesh door with a lock on it, and Kirsten pulled her gun and shot the lock apart.

She pushed the gates apart, and then, on the bike, drove down the steps, turning the tight corners, wondering how far she'd have to go in and underneath. She reached the platform and, as there were no trains, she dropped off the platform on the bike. There was a heavy thud. It wasn't straight, and it wasn't easy. Wooden slats across the base caused the bike to wobble. It kicked this way and that and then threw her off.

Her shoulder hit hard. She yelped in pain but Kirsten didn't have far to go, though. She thought she was at the edge of the Thames. It'd be in here, somewhere in here.

Kirsten met Goldsmith running out. He looked at her almost in disbelief. No chain around her neck. No bomb.

'How the hell did you do that?'

'Where is it?' she cried. 'Where's the bomb?'

He went for a gun, but she pulled hers first and shot him in the leg. It took his foot back, and he fell. She was in quick, kicking him hard and slapping her heel down on his hand. She kicked his gun away.

'Where is it?'

'You're too late,' he laughed. 'It's been activated.'

'I have time,' she said. 'You would have to get away. You would have to get . . .'

'My hovercraft's waiting. It will not be that long.'

Somebody was on the Thames waiting for him. Somebody was going to get him out of here. While all the police and all the ambulance crews were running around trying to sort out the other devices that had gone off, he would escape.

Kirsten dropped a hard boot onto the man's chin, knocking him out cold.

'If I'm going up, you bastard, you're going with me,' she said, and then turned and ran. There were occasional lights as she made her way down the tunnel. She was sure there were rats in the dark, but down here somewhere was a bomb.

Down here was the true device that was going to cause the actual pain. Not that what happened so far wasn't bloody enough. Somewhere there was a briefcase of XXYHD3, a packet load of boom that would be enough to half empty the Thames down and into the bunker below. There'd be no escape for the prime minister, the elected leader, the head of everything going wrong, according to Goldsmith, the one who should pay.

Kirsten felt her lungs burning. She'd tried to suck air as she ran, but she was beyond her limit. And then suddenly, there on the ground, a simple briefcase. She reached down, grabbed it, but it was heavier. Of course, it was heavier. Her briefcase had nothing in it. This one had it all. If it was an entire briefcase full, it'd be enough to blow half of London away, surely.

She thought about the small amount in the necklace and the damage it had done in the street. She thought about being blown off the lamppost. It was too much to comprehend.

Kirsten ran as hard as she could carrying the case. There was no point worrying about it getting jostled, there was no point worrying about it potentially going off by accident.

As she ran past Goldsmith, he raised his head. 'Three minutes,' he laughed. 'Three minutes.'

The laugh was from a demented man knowing he was going to die. She really shouldn't have, but Kirsten half stopped to lash a kick at the man's chin. *There's no failsafe*, she thought. *There's no failsafe. Of course not. Not for somebody like that.*

She could check, but that would be dead time. *What was she going to do with it, though?* she thought. *What could she do? How would she . . .?*

Kirsten couldn't worry about that now. She jumped back up onto the platform, hurrying up the stairs two at a time with the case. She fought to keep herself going. This was it. She either walked away from this a hero or she would be in a thousand unique pieces across whatever ruins were left.

Kirsten exited from the underground station out into the street near the banks of the Thames. *A minute and a half maybe, at most. What could she do?*

She looked left, nothing. Nothing there. Then, she turned her head right, five hundred metres along. Was that a fairground ride of some sort?

She turned and ran, desperation filling her every thought.

It was one of those giant seats, the bowls that they launched you up in, and then it caught before coming back down. One of those elasticated devices where people sat side by side like a bungee in reverse fired to the sky and then brought back down. Then they'd hang. But what if . . .?

She ran up to an empty platform with no one there. It had obviously been working not that long ago and had been cleared, but there was still power on to it. There was still electricity. She opened the cradle and threw the case inside. Kirsten turned and looked. She could set the launch sequence, but if she did that, would it work? Would she need to be in the cradle? She'd need to push the bomb out to the air. It didn't want to come back down with the cradle. She needed to be there to push it.

Kirsten didn't think; she just did. On the console, she pressed the button. When she heard the words, 'Five,' she skipped across and jumped into the cradle. 'Four.' She desperately looked for straps. 'Three.' She fought to get her arms in. 'Two.' Then she clicked the safety catch. 'One.' She reached right and grabbed the case. 'Fire,' came the words.

The seat she was sitting on, protected by a metal ball cage, took off towards the sky. She fought to put the case in front of her, tried to aim it between a gap in the metal safety grill. As the ball reached its height, Kirsten pushed the case as hard as she could.

It still had momentum. It still had the force it had been fired with. But the ball was now caught by the bungee ropes.

The ball fell backwards as the case continued upwards. The case exploded before Kirsten had returned on the bungee rope. She was just at the point of being sent back up when the bungee cord snapped from the force of the explosion.

Kirsten could hear windows exploding. She heard masonry fall, and an almighty bright light flew across the sky. A noise, as loud as she'd ever heard, sent her ears ringing. The ball swung around, and she spun on one cord.

Kirsten held tight, completely disorientated, and was then violently bashed to one side. Something snapped. And then she swung another direction, and the ball went round and round before it stopped.

Her eyes closed. She wasn't sure that her leg was in the right place. Something was screaming at her back, her shoulder was in agony, and she was sure she could feel blood dripping out of her mouth. But as much as she wanted to fight, extract herself from the wreckage, her body said no. Her eyes shut, and the darkness overtook her.

Chapter 25

Kirsten could hear a noise. It was close. Very close. It sounded like somebody breathing, slow and deliberate. Then there was a rustle like the page of a book turning. Everything was dark.

Slowly, she opened her eyes and was suddenly blinded. The light was strong, so she closed them again. Her shoulder hurt so badly. Her leg surely wasn't quite right. There are pains and aches everywhere. It felt as if somebody had picked her up and just dropped her from a large height, and she'd been left there struggling to raise herself.

She tried again to open her eyes. Slowly, the bright light diluted the shades. Cream. No, not cream. More like an off-white. There was a trolley in the corner. It had medical equipment on it. She rolled her head to the left and saw a man in the seat beside her. He was flicking through a novel, and her eyes tried to focus. She tried to ask who it was, but it just came out as some sort of moan.

'Good. You're awake.'

As soon as she heard the voice, she knew it was Justin Chivers. 'I'm sore,' she managed.

'You should be. I've never been in one of those fairground abominations myself, but I'm told that they don't fall apart, but then again, generally, they don't have large explosives being launched from them either. But you did it,' he said. 'You did it.'

Kirsten reached her hand over, and Justin put his hand in hers.

'We did it,' she said. The moment was cut off as the door opened. A man in a smart suit walked in. He was older. When her eyes focused, she saw who it was. She was ready to spit at him.

'Miss Stewart, a job well done, I see. I hope you're not injured too badly. The doctors seem to think you'll be up and on the move in a day or two, which is good. Obviously, we'll put the remuneration for your final bill over to you. We'll put this treatment on the house as well. I hope they're giving you excellent treatment. It's not cheap.'

'She's only just awake,' said Justin.

'Well, then she doesn't know how well she's done. The Prime Minister sends his thanks. I'd get him to greet you personally, but we don't let him talk to people from outside the service.'

Kristen wanted to say something brutal, wanted to have a comeback at the man, but she was just too sore. Instead, she lay back, and her eyes closed again. She wasn't sure how long she was asleep. When she woke up next, there was a woman sitting beside her bed.

'Long time,' said the woman. Kirsten recognised the face. Anna Hunt had been her boss. Anna had taught her a lot about the service, about being an agent. She was the one who had recommended her, and yet they'd fallen out on occasion. Kirsten was surprised to see her there.

'How are you doing?' asked Anna. Kirsten thought there was genuine affection in the question.

'Sore, but I'll be all right. Nothing broken,' they said. 'Severe bruising, terrible bruising, but nothing I won't recover from.'

'I heard you were overseas. I also heard you operated on your own in Alaska. That went down well. That's why Godfrey wanted you back in. I said, "No."'

'Really?'

'Really. You deserved to have rest. Enough on your plate with Craig.'

As Anna Hunt turned away, Kirsten realised there was regret there. Anna showed little emotion, and certainly, in the time that Kirsten had known her, she hadn't been one for sentiment. Things had changed, especially between Anna and Godfrey. It was hard. Once a close unit, Kirsten had detected the signs of anger within Anna towards him and his treatment of people.

'I've got a bit of bad news.'

'What?' asked Kirsten. She tried to raise herself on her pillows, but the pain was too much.

'Craig,' said Anna. 'He's left his treatment facility.'

'What do you mean, left? What, like signed himself out?'

'I don't know. I only heard an hour ago. Look, I thought I would come and tell you.'

'Why? Why is he gone? What's he . . .?'

'I don't know,' said Anna. 'Lie back. I thought you could try to find him, but you're in no condition. I spoke to your doctor. He said you would be at least a week in here, if not longer.'

'He's left because he was angry,' said Kirsten, becoming agitated. She felt the pain across her back. If she moved too suddenly, the bruising bit at her. 'He's never come to terms with it,' said Kirsten. 'Never. He needs more.'

'How do you come to terms with something like that? I've known many in the field who never have.'

'It wasn't the limbs,' said Kirsten. 'It was what he became.

He saw himself as lesser, useless.'

'I know because he was good. You don't get to work for Godfrey unless you're good,' said Anna.

She stood up. Kirsten saw she was dressed in jeans with a light jumper on and jacket. It wasn't her usual look. Anna was always immaculate, always well-tailored. Yes, sometimes, she wore shoes that would be more appropriate for being out on a mission. But Anna was always the perfect-looking spy, the operator that everyone else looked up to. Now she looked like she was going for a weekend in the country.

'Have you heard anything about him? Have you got any leads?'

'Nothing,' said Anna. 'I contacted the treatment facility, and they're not very clear about what's happened.'

'Then you need to get me up and out of here,' said Kirsten. 'I need to find out what's going on with him.'

'No, you don't. You'll stay here. You need to get better. Kirsten, you've done well this time,' she said. 'Done superb. I'll go find him.'

'What?'

'I said I'll go find him. He needs to come back in and get treatment. He needs to get on top of that anger.'

'It's difficult,' said Kirsten. 'He's changed. He's not . . .'

'I know it's not easy,' said Anna, spinning suddenly. 'A former agent, missing. He's angry. He's ripe pickings for other people to come to him. That's what they look for. They look for unsettlement. They look for someone with a grudge to bear against us in the service. He needs to come back in.'

The door opened, and Godfrey entered. 'There you are,' he said. 'A week's leave. There's enough clean-up going on at the moment with this. You really need a week's leave now.'

'It's clean up,' said Anna. 'You've got plenty of people within the service who can do clean-up. It's only a week. Besides, I may stop a bigger problem.'

Godfrey looked at Kirsten and over at Anna, and then back. 'You told her then,' he said.

'Of course, I have,' said Anna.

'He needs help,' said Kirsten. 'He needs to sort his mind out. He's . . .'

'He's a former agent,' said Godfrey, 'and we don't know where he is. And he's in an angry state of mind. He's a gross liability.'

'I know,' said Kirsten. 'Anna's just detailed it out for me. I know, but he's in a wheelchair. What's he going to do?'

Godfrey stopped and stared at Kirsten. He then turned and walked to the window.

'What's he going to do, Miss Hunt? Can you explain to Miss Stewart what he'll do?'

'If he's in an angry state of mind, he could be spoken to. He could be turned. He could give away information because he knows a lot of things. He could also still be used in the field. Hard to suspect a man in a wheelchair.'

'Come on,' said Kirsten. 'You can't be serious.'

'I'm very serious, Miss Stewart, and I'm monitoring the situation. One week it is,' Godfrey said to Anna. 'No longer. Be available.'

He walked to the door, opened it, then stopped and turned back to Kirsten. 'I wish you a restful week. Try to relax and get better.' He turned and closed the door behind him.

'He's not giving you much time to search, is he? I guess you've got plenty of work to do,' said Kirsten.

'No,' said Anna, 'it's one week or else he deems Craig to be a proper threat. Godfrey doesn't know many ways to deal with proper threats. You know, he acts in quite a brutal fashion. That's how we ended up in this mess.'

'Find him for me,' said Kirsten. 'Please.'

'Godfrey's right, you try to rest this week. It won't be easy, but if I haven't got him this week, you might try to find him in the weeks after. You need to be in shape. I'll let you know when I have something.'

Kirsten spent a fretful week sitting in a room trying to read, trying to watch television, trying to do anything else that would take her mind off Craig. She would scan the internet, seeing if there was any sign of him there, but there wasn't. There was a desperate effort, an attempt to manufacture some sort of plan from her bed, but she knew it was pointless. Anna was on it. Anna was on it, and Kirsten needed to trust. She was good. She was thorough. Anna was the cream.

A day passed, then two, then three, and no word from Anna. By the time the week had gone, Kirsten was worried. She hadn't got a number for Anna anymore. She tried contacting Godfrey. He'd gone incommunicado, not returning her calls. It was a damn cheek after what she'd just done. The press had been full of the attacks. There was mourning for the people who had died. The end count was thirty-three, all caught in blasts from the necklaces.

However, the larger bomb that went off, the one which many people heard throughout the greater London area, would've caused thousands to die, if not more. The TV carried the reconstruction work. It carried the horrific stories of people who had seen what looked like ordinary people with briefcases suddenly blow apart.

There was plenty of pain, but none of it hit home with

Kirsten. Her focus was purely on Craig, and on that front, she was getting nothing back. Kirsten flew up to Inverness exactly one week after Godfrey had told her to rest. When she arrived at Inverness, there was no one to meet her.

She'd hoped she might talk to Macleod, but he was off on a case, unavailable. She knew how that went. Detective Chief Inspector now. When the job called, you jerked to the pull of it.

Kirsten got a taxi and entered the flat that she'd shared with Craig. She was dog-tired, still sore from the bruising. She would take more time to recover.

Where was Anna Hunt? She hadn't spoken to Kirsten. She hadn't called. Kirsten didn't care, not tonight. The travel had taken more out of her than she thought. She ran a bath, hot and bubbly, and plonked herself in it. She was half an hour into lying there when she thought she heard the front door.

Slowly, she got out of the bath. Kirsten reached for a gun sitting beyond her towel. Once she had the weapon in her grasp, she wrapped the towel around her. She slowly opened the door and looked out into the living room. There was no one there. The front door was closed.

She went over and checked the locks. Nothing seemed out of place. Maybe she was just getting too edgy. She turned and saw it, a simple brown envelope on the table. A4 size. She picked it up. It read, 'Kirsten,' on the outside.

Carefully, she checked the rear, but everything said it was an ordinary envelope. She opened it delicately, then pulled out the small piece of paper inside. She held it, reading the four words written on it, tears streaming down her face. Anger was building up inside, and she wasn't sure at who or with whom, but it was coming in large doses.

She collapsed on the sofa, watched as the tears hit the paper she was holding, smudging the four words, words she would not forget.

'Sorry, Craig's gone rogue.'

Read on to discover the Patrick
Smythe series!

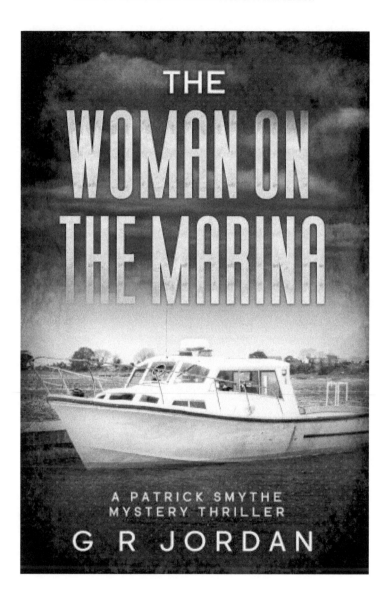

THE
WOMAN ON
THE MARINA

A PATRICK SMYTHE
MYSTERY THRILLER

G R JORDAN

Patrick Smythe is a former Northern Irish policeman who after suffering an amputation after a bomb blast, takes to the sea between the west coast of Scotland and his homeland to ply his trade as a private investigator. Join Paddy as he tries to work to his own ethics while knowing how to bend the rules he once enforced. Working from his beloved motorboat 'Craigantlet', Paddy decides to rescue a drug mule in this short story from the pen of G R Jordan.

Join G R Jordan's monthly newsletter about forthcoming releases and special writings for his tribe of avid readers and then receive your free Patrick Smythe short story.

Go to https://bit.ly/PatrickSmythe for your Patrick Smythe journey to start!

About the Author

GR Jordan is a self-published author who finally decided at forty that in order to have an enjoyable lifestyle, his creative beast within would have to be unleashed. His books mirror that conflict in life where acts of decency contend with self-promotion, goodness stares in horror at evil, and kindness blindsides us when we at our worst. Corrupting our world with his parade of wondrous and horrific characters, he highlights everyday tensions with fresh eyes whilst taking his methodical, intelligent mainstays on a roller-coaster ride of dilemmas, all the while suffering the banter of their provocative sidekicks.

A graduate of Loughborough University where he masqueraded as a chemical engineer but ultimately played American football, Gary had worked at changing the shape of cereal flakes and pulled a pallet truck for a living. Watching vegetables freeze at -40'C was another career highlight and he was also one of the Scottish Highlands "blind" air traffic controllers.

These days he has graduated to answering a telephone to people in trouble before telephoning other people to sort it out.

Having flirted with most places in the UK, he is now based in the Isle of Lewis in Scotland where his free time is spent between raising a young family with his wife, writing, figuring out how to work a loom and caring for a small flock of chickens. Luckily, his writing is influenced by his varied work and life experience as the chickens have not been the poetical inspiration he had hoped for!

You can connect with me on:

🜨 https://grjordan.com

⬛ https://facebook.com/carpetlessleprechaun

Subscribe to my newsletter:

✉ https://bit.ly/PatrickSmythe

Also by G R Jordan

G R Jordan writes across multiple genres including crime, dark and action adventure fantasy, feel good fantasy, mystery thriller and horror fantasy. Below is a selection of his work. Whilst all books are available across online stores, signed copies are available at his personal shop.

Implosion (A Kirsten Stewart Thriller #11)
https://grjordan.com/product/implosion
Secret service operatives being despatched. An unknown group with no known agenda. Can Kirsten discover the ringleader before the service is torn apart?

Whilst looking for her damaged lover, Kirsten Stewart is hired by Godfrey to root out a terror group which is striking at the heart of the service. Assassinations of key individuals and bombings of secret locations has the intelligence world in a frenzy. Kirsten must trust no one as she hunts the slightest of clues to these clandestine attackers. But when Godfrey is targeted, panic sets in, and Kirsten wonders if the service will crumble.

How sturdy the foundations built on secrets and lies...

The First Minister: Past Mistakes Trilogy #1

https://grjordan.com/product/the-first-minister

A cryptic note to a long-retired policeman. A clergyman stabbed by a masked figure in public. Can Macleod and McGrath find the story behind the panic as it becomes open season on the church?

When a note is delivered to a care home on the isle of Harris, it seems to be a joke in bad taste until the prediction comes true. As more notes are sent and clergy die, Macleod and his team have to open up a wall of silence regarding the reason for such hatred. In a trail that leads across all of Scotland, the DCI finds something more unpalatable than the murders before him.

A wall of silence can only be broken by blood!

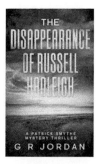

**The Disappearance of Russell Hadleigh
(Patrick Smythe Book 1)**

https://grjordan.com/product/the-disappearance-of-russell-hadleigh

**A retired judge fails to meet his golf
partner. His wife calls for help while
running a fantasy play ring. When
Russians start co-opting into a fairly-
traded clothing brand, can Paddy untangle the strands
before the bodies start littering the golf course?**

In his first full novel, Patrick Smythe, the single-armed former
policeman, must infiltrate the golfing social scene to discover
the fate of his client's husband. Assisted by a young starlet
of the greens, Paddy tries to understand just who bears a
grudge and who likes to play in the rough, culminating in a
high stakes showdown where lives are hanging by the reaction
of a moment. If you love pacey action, suspicious motives and
devious characters, then Paddy Smythe operates amongst your
kind of people.

Love is a matter of taste but money always demands more of
its suitor.

Milton Keynes UK
Ingram Content Group UK Ltd.
UKHW040854110923
428455UK00001B/28